ROAM

Also by Erik Therme

IF SHE DIES
I KNOW YOU
KEEP HER CLOSE
RESTHAVEN
MORTOM

ROAM

THECKER BOOKS

ISBN-13: 978-0692797075
ISBN-10: 0692797076

Dedicated to my Parnell crew:
Steve & Jen
Chad
Neva
Rik

ONE

If someone had asked Sarah Cate what she wanted for her twenty-first birthday, her response would have been this: a quiet, romantic night out with her boyfriend. It didn't matter if it was dinner and a movie or a drive under the stars—all that mattered was that they were together.

"Are you done yet?" Matt yelled.

She was still trying to figure out how she had ended up squatting in a ditch in the middle of nowhere. Now all she wanted was some toilet paper and her cell phone. Preferably in that order.

She swiftly finished her business and made her way back across the road. Matt was sprawled out in the passenger seat of her car with the door opened. His head was against the headrest, but his eyes were on her.

"It's getting dark," she said, batting at a firefly. "Can you try your cell phone again?"

"I already told you there's no reception this far out. Maybe if you'd remembered *your* phone, we wouldn't be stuck here right now."

"That makes sense," she muttered. Her hands went to her hips. "Can you at least try to sober up so we can figure out what's wrong with my car?"

"I am not drunk," he said, holding up a finger. It weaved and bobbed in the air as he climbed out. "I can hold my liquor, okay? I know my limits."

"Fine. Whatever. I just want to get out of here. Do you want *me* to pop the hood and take a look?"

For some reason he found this hysterically funny and burst into laughter. It quickly turned into a coughing fit, and she whapped him between the shoulders hard enough to sting her palm.

His coughs shifted over to dry heaves and began to taper off. He didn't look good. His cheeks were completely drained of color and tiny beads of sweat peppered his forehead.

"Matt?"

He let out a small belch and wiped his mouth on his sleeve. "What?"

"Maybe it's the thing with the antifreeze. The radiator. My mom says she keeps seeing green puddles in our driveway where I park. Maybe it's low on fluid and the engine overheated."

"Let's leave the guy stuff for me to figure out," Matt said, pulling the latch and raising the hood. A cloud of smoke filled the air and he took a step back. "Whoa."

"Well?" she asked.

His face wrinkled in thought. It seemed to say *This is a very profound question you have asked of me, and I will take it under very serious consideration*. It was the same expression he had when picking out a movie or deciding on something from a menu.

"I think it's the radiator," he said in small voice. "Lucky guess."

Baby-sitting, Sarah thought angrily. *Baby-sitting on my birthday.*

Two weeks she had been dreaming of this night: a birthday to remember. Everything had been fine until he had talked her into stopping at a party for a quick drink after they had eaten. It was her night, and she had still gone out of her way to make him happy.

"Good Little Girlfriend," she said under her breath. She dug out her cigarettes and promised herself again she would not buy another pack when they were gone.

"This is insane," said Matt. He was standing in the middle of the road with one hand frozen halfway through his hair. "Where the hell is everybody?"

She looked around, not understanding. "What are you talking about?"

"This road should be *hopping*. It's the most traveled road between Norridge and Centerview."

On this she secretly agreed—everyone knew the interstate between the two towns took an additional fifteen minutes—but she wasn't about to give him the satisfaction of admitting it.

"I give up," he said, lowering himself to the pavement. "Just leave me for the buzzards and crows. And tell my mother that I love her . . . and remember to feed my fish . . ."

She crossed her arms. This was the part where she was supposed to laugh and everything would magically return to normal. She knew the routine by heart. But he wasn't going to get off that easily—no way in hell. This was her birthday (the freakin BIG one, at that), and it was being destroyed right in front of her eyes.

"Why don't you go sit in the car?" she said.

He lay back and draped an arm over his forehead. "I'm too drunk to do anything, remember?"

"Come on," she said, trying to keep her voice light. "Your clothes are going to get dirty."

She shot a glance at the curve behind him. A car speeding around it wouldn't have time to see someone sprawled across the pavement, let alone have time to stop. Kuennen Road wasn't only a well-known shortcut; it was also a popular road for speeding.

"Matt, come over here and help me fix this."

He's going to get run over, she thought, dumbfounded. *What a perfect ending to a perfect evening.*

"Matt, this isn't funny!"

She knew he wasn't going to budge—not until she went out and got him. Worse yet, she also knew that *he* knew this as well. If a car splattered him, it would be her fault, because she didn't do what she was supposed to do. It always had to be on his terms. When they went out to eat, it was up to her to choose the restaurant, but only after: "What do you think? Chinese or Mexican food?" At the video store, *he* would pick out two movies and then say: "These both look good . . . you decide which one." Her personal favorite was the first time she had suggested a theater movie and received back: "Yeah, that looks pretty good, but it's a half-hour longer than this other one, and it starts fifteen minutes later. Plus, that type of movie is just as good on DVD, not like this other one that really needs to be seen on the big screen. But hey, if that's really the one you want to see . . ." The conversation might have been funny if it had been the gentle teasing that all couples did to each other, but he had been dead serious. He had weighed the pros and cons, formulated theories and opinions, and made a case. Just like a lawyer to the jury: *These are all the facts, and I know you'll use common sense and make the right decision.*

"I'm going to wait inside the car," she called out. "Okay?"

There was no reply. For a horrible second she thought he had passed out.

"Matt!"

"I can't get up . . . or speak . . . in . . . complete . . . sentences . . ."

She pushed all her emotions into a ball and shoved it to the side the best she could. The forgotten cigarette dropped from her fingers as she walked over to him, hating herself for it.

"Come on," she said, reaching down and grabbing his elbow. It was a futile effort, but she struggled with him nonetheless. "Work *with* me," she said with a grunt.

"I'll work something with you," he grinned, grabbing her wrist and pulling her down into a clumsy hug.

"Let me go!"

"What?" he asked innocently.

She twisted and jerked as the smell of alcohol from his breath doused her face. Then she heard it: the low, deep rumble of a muffler from beyond the curve.

She tried to push him away. "Matt," she snapped, "there's a car—"

He kissed her sloppily and she lost it; her fingernails that had been so carefully filed and painted turned into claws, burrowing into his stomach.

"Hey," he said with a faint laugh. "That kind of—"

She had a perfect view of his face when the pain finally registered, and then he wasn't only releasing her—he was *throwing* her.

"A car!" she shouted, scrambling over to the side of the road. "There's a car coming, you stupid ass!"

She cupped a hand over her mouth, tracking the curve for headlights or sounds. There was nothing. She clambered to her feet as Matt came at her.

"You cut me," he said in a shaky voice, holding up his shirt.

"I thought—"

"Look at this!"

She glanced at the three red lines above his belly button and decided she didn't care. It was his own damn fault and she wasn't taking responsibility for him anymore.

"I'm sorry," she said. "I thought I heard a car."

"Where, huh? I don't see anything!"

His face was a grotesque mixture of fury and rage, and in that moment, Sarah was afraid. He was drunk and pissed off and the situation was getting out of control. She took a step back and his hand latched on to her arm. Panic seized her by the throat.

This is not happening, she told herself.

He raised his fist. His upper lip was curled back into a snarl, and in that split second, Sarah understood what had happened: a case had been made and she had been convicted. She had hurt him and now he was going to hurt her.

It was as simple as that.

His fist whirled past her and slammed into the car. She jerked free and backed away in a series of harried steps.

"Shit," he said, just under his breath. His head was lowered, and his palms were pressed flat against the trunk of the car. Between his thumbs sat a small, shadowed dent.

"My horrible temper," he offered, and then pushed out a loud sigh. "I suppose that makes me a bad person, huh? Losing it like that?"

Sarah said nothing, and when his eyes swung toward her she realized he wanted a response. It wasn't rhetorical.

"No," she whispered.

A dark freeze came over his face, hardening his features. He seemed to still be questioning her: *Are you sure that's your final answer?* She found herself unable to look away, only because she didn't recognize the guy standing there.

"Work has been . . . difficult these last few weeks. You just don't know the pressures, Sarah. Not all of us can work part-time and live at home like you. Consider yourself lucky."

Her mouth opened, but only a small fit of air crept out. If he was supposed to be making an apology, it wasn't working. If he was trying to push her buttons, he was working straight from the manual.

"Just excuses," he added. "Things just haven't gone as planned lately. Like tonight. And now this has probably ruined your birthday present. I was planning on tonight being 'the night.' And for that, I'm sorry. But maybe it's not too late? You know . . . to start over?"

A slanted smile touched his lips, and for a moment she was so taken aback she couldn't speak. After everything that had been said and done, he was still trying to get laid. The path of the night wasn't going to end up where he wanted it, so the obvious solution was to admit he had been an ass and get things back on track. She knew he didn't believe it, but he knew enough to say it. This was his way. Again, if you examined the facts, there was only one reasonable conclusion to draw: they had been dating for three months; they had gone out for a nice dinner; it was her birthday.

She had a way as well. It was something along the lines of *No way was this asshole ever going to touch her again*. It didn't matter if she was with someone for ten years or ten minutes; all that mattered was that it felt right. There was no agenda.

Almost shyly: "What do you think, Sarah?"

She forced herself to look at him. He was playing the part beautifully: shoulders slumped, hands crammed into his pockets . . . even his head was bowed slightly, puppy dog eyes watching and waiting for a pat on the head. *Come on*, they said. *Be a sport.*

"I'm sorry," she said.

"Don't apologize," he said with a small smile. "There's still time—"

"Sorry I ever *met* you," she finished.

It was probably the cheesiest, most clichéd thing she could have said, but it still felt good. Good Little Girlfriends didn't talk back.

"Sarah, you don't mean that."

He was grinning, but his eyes were two narrow slits. They told another story. They asked again if that was her final answer.

"You shouldn't joke about that," he said. He began to slowly roll up his sleeves. "It's not funny."

This is wrong, a voice inside her spoke up. *You need to get away from this situation right now.*

"We just need to get moving," she stammered as he moved toward her. "We can figure out the rest later."

His hands clamped down on her shoulders and she gave a startled cry.

"If you broke up with me," he said, his fingers digging into her skin, "I'd make you so sorry you'd never forget it. I'd follow you to the ends of the earth, and you'd never have one moment of peace because you'd always be looking over your shoulder, wondering when the day would finally come that I'd appear out of thin air and drag you into your own living nightmare. Do you get me?"

"Matt," she rasped, "I didn't—"

"Kidding!" he laughed, and gave her a firm shake. He backed away with his hands raised. "I'm sorry. I was just playing. But you see how horrible that was? Jokes go too far. Just like you saying you wished you never met me. Yeah?"

She nodded furiously as tears began to sting her eyes. He gingerly touched her cheek, and it took all her strength not to pull away.

"I didn't mean to scare you that bad," he said. "Sarah, you're the best thing I've got right now, and the last thing I want to do is push you away. Everything will be fine once we get back to my place. You'll see. I'm going to go check out the car now, okay?"

Somehow she managed another nod, and the moment his back was turned she grabbed on to the car handle to steady herself. She told herself she was okay; everything was going to be fine. She was going to get through this and maybe never look back. Ever.

"Radiator's probably still too hot to be opened," he said, "but I got plenty of piss to spare. Gotta go *real* bad."

Sarah blinked stupidly in his direction.

"It's a guy trick," he explained. "Piss works the same as water inside a radiator. When the radiator overheats and you don't have any water, you just piss into it to fill it back up. Then you're back in business."

She opened her mouth to tell him not to *pee* into her car . . . but something inside her clicked. It was time for her to leave. It was such a simple idea that she didn't know why it had taken so long to come to her. The road was deserted, but there were houses scattered along it. Farm houses with people and phones.

"Matt?"

It came out as no more than a croak, immediately lost within the rustling trees and screeching crickets. She swallowed and cleared her throat.

"Matt?" she said again louder.

He stepped out from behind the raised hood. There was a dab of dirt on his chin, and he was using the corner of his shirt to wipe his hands. The shirt alone probably cost more than everything she was wearing, and he was smearing oil and grime all across it. It was almost funny.

"Yeah, babe?" he asked.

A benevolent smile touched the corners of his mouth, and for a moment Sarah found herself stuck. He looked like the guy she had started the evening with again—the guy she had first met at the café who tripped over her shopping bags and spilled coffee all over himself. He had laughed so hard she had been unable to stop from joining in. It had been his smile that had baited her into dropping her phone number in his direction. It was warm and inviting, and yes—it could light up a whole damn room.

"What's up?" he asked gently. He literally looked like he would have swallowed drain cleaner for her if asked. And that was the problem. Five minutes ago he was on the verge of smacking her, and now he was Mr. Nice Guy?

"I just remembered that there's an old family friend that lives in a house about a mile from here," she lied. "It's just down the road. I was thinking I would walk down there and ask to use the phone."

His hands stopped and his smile dimmed. Sarah forced herself not to swallow.

"Why would you want to do that?" he asked. There was no trace of anything in his face now. "Don't you trust me to take care of this, Sarah?"

"It's not that," she said, all at once aware of the small earthquakes erupting inside her hands. She stuffed them behind her back. "We just haven't seen a car yet, and we might not see one for a long time. I mean, who's to say they'd even stop? Not everyone stops for people in trouble, especially in the middle of a deserted road. I just . . . I thought that . . ."

His eyes crawled over her suspiciously, and she told herself to keep it under control.

"You don't have to do anything, Matt. You can stay and keep working on the car, and as soon as I call someone, I'll come back."

He took a step in her direction and she exploded into tears.

"I can't do this," she sobbed. It came out in a loud burst, startling her as much as him. "Please don't . . . please stay there. Please don't yell at me anymore. Please . . ."

She wept blindly into her hands, knowing that he was storming toward her. She could hear the slap of his shoes against the pavement, could feel the barrage of fists that was sure to come. She had lost it and now he was done with her. No more Mr. Nice Guy; no more Good Little Girlfriend.

When she dared to look, she saw that he was in the same place. A troubled frown was etched across his lips.

"My God, Sarah," he whispered. "I had no idea what I'd done to you."

His words were so soft that she was barely catching them, and she tried to shift her breathing down to a lower gear.

"I don't know what to say," he choked, then placed a hand across his mouth. "This is my fault. This whole mess of a night."

They stared at each other through the fading light, two figures not speaking or moving. Three hours ago she had picked him up in her car, the evening ahead of them brimming with excitement and anticipation. They had been Matt and Sarah: boyfriend and girlfriend. It was her twenty-first birthday and everything was going to be perfect.

"Whatever you want to do, Sarah," he said. "If you feel better doing this, I completely understand."

Shame and guilt threatened to creep up inside her, and it took all of her strength to force them back down. Too much had been said to even begin to sort it out.

"I would never hurt you," Matt said roughly, but the anger was directed at himself. "And I'll never forgive myself if this causes problems in our relationship."

"I didn't mean for . . . I just want to help. I didn't mean to freak out—"

"Just be careful. Make sure to walk on the side of the road, and if I do get the car working and you hear me coming, be sure to raise your arms high in the air so I can see you."

"Okay," she said, slightly confused. The conversation seemed to have taken on the tone of a formal business meeting.

"I just hope you're right about that house. If not, it's ten miles back to town, and once you lose the last of the light, you'll only have the moon to work with." He let out a small, almost polite laugh. "Of course, if you don't find the house, you'll be turning around and coming right back."

Sarah dropped her eyes. "Of course."

"Watch your feet," he continued, "because those sandals aren't going to be kind to you. They're prime material for blisters, especially on a hard surface like this. But it shouldn't be a problem because you're not going very far."

"No," she answered in a glassy whisper.

"And if I were you, I'd be skeptical about accepting a ride if someone does come by. Someone might drive past me and then stop for you. After all, you're a young, beautiful girl walking alone down a dark, deserted road, and I won't be there to protect you if something bad happens. I'm not trying to scare you, Sarah, but these are just facts. People get murdered and raped in this world every single day."

Sarah shot a glance down the road, squinting into the wind. There was nothing inviting about the scenario. The surrounding fields were bustling with strange noises and sounds. A thousand hiding places for the criminally insane were laid out ahead of her. Every horror movie she had watched came back to her, reminding her of what never to do. And number one was never be a young girl alone in the dark.

Stay or go. Go or stay. Either way was impossible.

She turned to say something and abruptly stopped. Matt was watching her, his face serious and attentive, but she had seen it. It had been so small and fleeting that she could have easily convinced herself it was imagined, but there was no doubt. The grin on his lips had been wiped away a millisecond too late.

"What are you thinking?" he asked somberly.

She carefully reached into her pocket. The key ring jingled in her hand as she wrestled off the ignition key, and when she held it out to him, there was no mistaking the movement of his lips: they coiled into a tight frown. His arm rose slowly and she dropped the key into his hand.

"I don't think you want to do this, Sarah," he said coldly.

She began to walk away, watching him over her shoulder as she went. His arm was still frozen in the air; if there had been a revolver in his hand, he would have looked like a gunfighter after the draw. Her heart began to race, keeping a steady beat with her footsteps. Now he was going to come after her. Her hands tightened around the strap of her purse.

"If something bad happens," he called after her, "I'm not taking responsibility for it."

Once she made it around the curve she would be out of sight, and it would all be better. Then she could . . . could *what*? Walk the whole ten miles back into town? She knew there were people in the world that could run a four-minute mile, so the best she could hope to do on foot was maybe fifteen minutes a mile? Right there would be almost two and a half hours of panic-stricken, trauma-forming, alone-in-the-dark footwork. The sensible part of her said it wasn't too late to turn around and forget the whole thing. Surely a car would be by soon and they could both get a lift. Then she wouldn't be alone with Matt or alone with a stranger.

"You don't want to do this, you *bitch*!" Matt yelled.

She shut her eyes, missing a step and almost tangling her feet.

She was walking.

[2]

The metallic black monster barreled across the pavement, eating up the road and belching blue smoke. A squirrel scrambling across a tree branch froze and watched as the machine rumbled past.

"Curve," said Mark, pointing at the road ahead.

Kevin nodded thoughtfully and stepped on the gas pedal. "Got it."

"Uh, most people brake *before* they drive into a sharp turn."

"Really? How boring for them."

Kevin took the curve without slowing, sending them both to one side in their seats. He tightened his grip on the wheel as the Camaro straightened. Pushing the boundaries of the road was one of the few vices he still allowed himself, and it never got old.

"Maniac," Mark said, knocking a cigarette into his hand.

"No smoking in here."

"I forgot. No smoking, farting, or breathing heavy inside the car. God forbid that something should happen to the cheap vinyl interior."

"Exactly."

"But yet you have no qualms about endangering our lives or running the car off the road. Makes perfect sense."

"It's an enigma," Kevin agreed, but eased off the accelerator. Today wasn't a day to take unnecessary chances. Not until midnight, anyway. After midnight, all bets were off.

"Parent advisory warning," said Mark.

"Huh?"

Kevin slowed the Camaro as they passed a car parked in the gravel next to the road. The hood was propped open, but no one seemed to be around.

"Probably some college kids faking a breakdown," Mark said with a yawn. "Right now, some dude is getting lucky in a nearby ditch."

"Maybe." Kevin tromped on the gas pedal and watched the gauge sink a notch. "I don't remember it being there on the way to the alley."

"What did you bowl again?"

"Stuff it."

"No, I forgot," Mark said with a grin. "Fifty-two? Fifty-six? Your name will forever be immortalized with the great bowlers of the Norridge Coral Lanes. And now that our senior year of high school is safely behind us, you can finally go full-time pro."

Kevin didn't hear; his eyes were tracking the girl that was walking down the side of the road. She was out of the Camaro's headlights in a matter of seconds, and without thinking he brought the car to a stop.

"Really?" Mark sighed.

"Maybe that was her car back there. She may need a ride."

Mark looked over his shoulder. "She's never going to get in here with us."

Kevin fumbled the Camaro into reverse and backed up until they were next to her. "Hello."

The girl hurried past without glancing up. He shifted back into drive and tapped on the gas pedal until they were creeping beside her. She was moving briskly now, staring into the ground and clutching a purse under one arm. Kevin snapped on the dome light so she could see them clearly.

"Can we offer you a ride?" he asked.

She shook her head. He told himself there was no way he was going to make this happen. For all she knew they were psychos, cruising around looking for young women to molest . . . which was the exact reason he didn't want to leave her out there. *He* knew they were okay; all he had to do was convince her.

"You shouldn't be out here alone," Kevin told her. "A lot of idiot kids tear around this road at night."

"Like us," Mark said under his breath. Kevin elbowed him in the ribs.

"We can give you a lift into town. Do you live in Centerview?"

"Come on, man," Mark whispered. "Let's just—"

"It's a long walk," Kevin said. "About fifteen miles."

The girl lifted her head and stopped. Kevin felt a flutter in his stomach as their eyes touched. She didn't look familiar, and he knew he would have remembered her. Attractive was an understatement; this girl deserved a *stunning* award.

"You saw a car?" she asked.

"Yeah, about a mile or so back—"

"Why didn't you pick up the guy that was with it?"

"We didn't see anyone. Was someone supposed to be there?"

"My boyfriend," she said in a strong voice. "He was probably under the car looking at it or something, but I'm sure he saw you. He's a mechanic, so he would know the make and model of your car. He probably got your license plate number too. He remembers stuff like that."

"Do you want us to go back and get him?" Kevin asked. "I'd be more than happy to pick him up and then come back for you."

Her brow creased as she studied him. Mark had lost all interest and was picking at a scab on his elbow.

"I have pepper spray," she said, slipping a hand into her purse. "I'm just warning you in case you try anything."

Kevin nodded. "Fair enough."

She lingered a moment longer, her chest rapidly rising and falling. "Fine."

Kevin slid out and held open the car door. A scowl took hold of her face as she studied the cramped back seats.

"I can kick Mark into the back," he said. Mark perked up and Kevin shot him a *Say-one-word-and-you'll-be-the-one-walking* glare.

"It's fine," she said stiffly. She climbed inside, and her hand went back into her purse the second she was settled. Kevin lowered the driver seat into place, got in, and gently shut the door behind him.

"Now we'll get your boyfriend," he said, meeting her eyes in the rearview mirror.

"He must have gotten a ride," she replied after a brief hesitation. "Just please take me back to town."

"Really, it's no bother—"

"Please, just go. I need to get home."

He paid her a final glance in the rearview mirror before slowly driving away, mindful of the fifty-five-mile-an-hour speed limit sign that loomed off to one side.

[3]

Sarah spotted the police cruiser as soon as they turned down her street; it was parked where Kirby's pickup should have been.

"Right here," she stammered. "Here."

The car shuddered to a stop and she was pushing on the seat before the door was open. Her brain was already churning out a hundred scenarios: there had been an accident . . . someone had tried to break in . . . Matt had called her house and her mother had called the police . . .

She was halfway up the driveway when the front door opened and two officers stepped out. They were smiling and talking amongst themselves.

"What happened?" Sarah choked.

The officers looked up in surprise. The one nearest to her spoke: "Are you Sarah?"

She nodded. "Is my mom okay?"

"Yes. She's inside. There's been a little excitement, but it's all over now."

"Is it . . . was it something to do with Kirby?"

The officers exchanged a glance—a look passed by partners who had experienced something too many times to count. Of course it was Kirby. It was stupid to ask.

"I'm sorry you had to come out here," Sarah said. "Thank you."

"Like I told your mother, call us if you need to. Don't hesitate. That's why we're here."

"Thank you," she said again.

She waited until the officers were inside the cruiser before scurrying up the steps and opening the door. The inside of the house was warm as always; the air-conditioning more illusion than reality. Above the thermostat was a piece of masking tape that read: *Do not turn below 80*. Kirby had placed it there after moving in and taking over the electric bill.

"Sarah?"

Her mother was framed in the kitchen door with both hands clasped beneath her bosom. A paper-thin nightgown clung to her body, and her breasts were faintly visible underneath.

"Sarah, what are you doing home?"

"What happened?"

"Happened?" her mother asked. "I was doing some dishes. In the kitchen."

"Why were the police here?"

A perfunctory smile appeared on her mother's thin lips. "Did you see a police car on your way here? They were probably just out patrolling the neighborhood—"

"I know they were in here, Mother," Sarah said evenly. "I met them as they were going out the door. They were . . . God, Mom; your boobs are showing through. They were smiling when they left."

"Oh," her mother replied quietly, slipping an absent glance at herself before crossing her arms. "I didn't realize. How stupid of me."

Her mother turned and disappeared into the kitchen. Sarah followed and found her at the sink, pushing up the sleeves of her gown.

"Tell me what happened," Sarah said.

"Kirby and I had a small disagreement," she answered, mechanically washing the dishes. "That's all. Our voices may have gotten a little loud. The stupid neighbors . . ."

Sarah let out a sharp breath. It was just the usual nonsense, nothing more.

"The neighbors need to mind their own business," her mother finished. "It wasn't like he . . . we weren't throwing things or anything. It was nothing."

"It must have been *something*. The police were here."

A plate clanked inside the sink. "You don't understand these things, Sarah. They're complicated."

"Then tell me. Tell me what there is to understand."

Her mother shook her head and picked up a towel. "It was my fault. Kirby was in a bad mood to begin with, and it was my fault."

"How was it your fault?"

"He was told he may lose his job," her mother said. "Work has been slow at the factory, and the foreman is looking to lay off some people."

Sarah held her mouth shut. Kirby had only been with them six months and had already gone through three jobs.

"It's only because it's been slow at the factory," her mother said with a touch of petulance. "Martha Jennings told me before I heard it from Kirby. Her grandson knows one of the managers there, and I picked it up in normal conversation from her. About how slow it is down there."

"And why is that your fault?" Sarah asked.

Her mother exhaled and looked into her hands.

"Mom, *how* is that your fault?"

"So hot in here," her mother said, pushing open the window above the sink. "Air conditioning must be on the blink."

"Mom—"

"I asked Kirby how he was going to pay his portion of the bills if he got laid off. You know things are tight, and when he moved in, I quit working at the laundry, but without his extra income . . ."

She trailed off. Sarah didn't need her to finish.

"He got pissed, Mom," she said. "He got pissed and started yelling."

"I shouldn't have asked. With all the other stuff going on in his life, the last thing he needs—"

"Don't do that," Sarah said, gritting her teeth. "Don't defend that *asshole*."

"Sarah!" her mother gasped.

"You know it's true. All he does is eat our food and drink away most of the money. You really think he cares for us? Cares for you?"

Her mother tried to speak, but only a small sound escaped her mouth. Tears began to shine her eyes.

"Why do you do this to yourself?" Sarah asked with a thick sigh. She didn't understand why her mother bothered to date at all; none of the men lasted more than a brief snatch of time.

"I'm scared," her mother said in a thin voice. She sat at the table and wiped at her cheeks. "I know it's selfish and wrong of me, but I can't help it. I . . . don't want to be alone when you're gone. I don't want to be alone again."

"Gone? What are you talking about?"

But she knew. Most of her friends had already moved out of the house, if not the city or the state. But there she was, still living under the same roof in the house where she grew up. It was something that never came up between them but was always in the back of Sarah's mind.

"And with things going so well between you and Matt," her mother said, "I figure it's only a matter of time before . . . you know."

"Before what?" Sarah asked, confused.

Her mother smiled. "Matt's a keeper, Sarah. He's got a secure job, he's nice looking, and he's pleasant to be around. Everything anyone could need or want in a man."

"He's not," Sarah said. "He's just like the rest of them. I found that out tonight the hard way."

"Where is Matt?" her mother asked, looking past her into the living room. "Is he outside, waiting in the car? You shouldn't keep him waiting, Sarah."

Sarah took in a breath. "Matt's not here. And I don't think he'll be coming around anymore."

Her mother's face was static with shock. "What are you saying?"

"I think . . . Matt and I are done."

"What did you *do*?" her mother snapped so loudly it made Sarah flinch. It was the wrong thing to say, and at that moment Sarah felt a jab of hatred toward her mother like never before. There was no question where the Good Little Girlfriend song and dance had been learned. Drunk, stupid, deadbeat . . . it didn't matter. It was up to the Cate women to shoulder the burden of the relationship and absorb the guilt and blame.

"Answer me, Sarah."

"Matt was . . . he tried to . . ." The words stuck in her mouth as her thought process overheated from anger. What did he do exactly? He kissed her in the road; he *almost* hit her; he made her feel like shit.

"Sarah, couples have spats, but they don't abandon each other because of them. They don't fly off the handle at every small thing that happens."

"It wasn't like that," Sarah said, finding her voice. "It wasn't some dumb argument about where to eat or what movie to watch—"

"You learn to make sacrifices," her mother continued. "Sometimes it's hard, but you have to learn to make the other person happy. To put the other person before yourself."

"I knew you wouldn't understand," Sarah said, rising from the table.

"Sarah, don't throw this away. I won't let you blow this over some dumb tiff."

"It wasn't some dumb *tiff* and it's not your decision. It's not . . . this has nothing to do with you! Why are you doing this?"

"Will you listen to me?" her mother said as she stood. "I'm just trying to help you understand that someday—"

"Someday *what*?" Sarah shouted. "That if I learn to keep my mouth shut and my legs open, I can live like you?"

The slap came fast and hard.

"Oh, Sarah," her mother whispered, looking at her hand, which was still raised. "I didn't . . . I—I—"

Sarah stumbled away from the table, knocking over the chair as tears began to blind her vision.

"I didn't mean it," her mother choked, reaching out to her.

It was the last thing Sarah heard before running through the living room and out the front door.

[4]

"You coming to Jeff's game tomorrow?" Mark asked.

Kevin shrugged and drummed his fingers against the steering wheel. "Probably not. I'm pretty burned out on poker, and my cash flow is practically non-existent at the moment."

"Loser. And to think I was feeling bad for bailing out on you so early tonight. But I gotta go please that woman of mine. You know how it is. Oh, wait. You don't."

"Get outta here."

Mark slammed the door, stuck his head through the window, and let out a giant, flammable belch.

"I can get that shit at my house," Kevin said irritably. "And I'm gonna tear up that fake I.D. the next time I see you try and use it. Then you'll be shit outta luck."

"Don't pick up any hitchers on your way home."

"Whatever."

He squealed the tires as he pulled away, then sucked in a quick breath when a police cruiser turned onto the street from the opposite direction. To his surprise, the driver only paid him a casual glance as they passed. Usually it was a full-blown stare, because with a Camaro he *must* be out tearing up the roads and causing trouble.

"Good old delinquent days," he mumbled, catching sight of a scuff mark on the glove box. He rubbed it away with his thumb and straightened just as someone ran into the road in front of him. Both feet went into the brake pedal and the Camaro screeched to a halt as the person staggered over and opened the passenger side door. It was the girl from earlier.

"You almost hit me," she choked and then burst into tears. Before he could speak, she fell into the seat and slammed the door behind her. "Can you please go?"

"Go?"

"Just *drive*. Anywhere but here."

Kevin stepped on the gas. The Camaro bucked and coughed and then smoothed out. The girl was still crying, but it was a soft sound. Her hands moved in quick, jerky swipes as she wiped at her tears.

"Are you okay?" he asked.

She shook her head. His eyes wandered across her tank top, and he looked away guiltily as he saw her bra strap.

"You're not hurt, are you?"

He paused at the end of the street, waiting to see if she was going to give him any direction.

"I'm not hurt," she said quietly.

He crossed the intersection and kept his speed at twenty miles an hour, trying to draw out the road. The good news was that she seemed to have the tears under control; the bad news was that she wasn't supplying any information.

"Do you need me to take you somewhere?" he asked. "I'm more than happy to."

He watched as she dug into her purse and pulled out a pack of cigarettes. Something seemed to dawn on her face and she poked them back inside.

"Go ahead," he told her.

She regarded him suspiciously.

"Really," he said with a small nod.

She took out a cigarette and lit it with a shaky hand. Her face began to twitch, and his stomach tightened in anticipation of more tears. Instead, she let out a hearty sneeze and wiped her nose with the back of her hand.

"Bless you."

Her brow creased, and he turned back toward the road, determined not to speak anymore. Everything out of his mouth seemed to be upsetting her.

"You must think I'm nuts," she said, but without much conviction.

"Not at all."

She tossed the cigarette out the window and he caught a splash of orange in the rearview mirror as it struck the pavement. They were running out of road and she still wasn't giving him any direction. He looked at her. Her hands were trembling. She didn't seem to notice or care that he was watching, and he found himself unwilling to turn away. She was older than he was; he was sure of that now.

"What happened to your friend?" she asked.

He jerked his gaze back to the road. "I, uh, dropped him off at his house. It's actually just a few blocks from yours."

He could feel her watching *him* now, and he was suddenly aware of every little thing on his face: the stubble he had neglected to shave that morning, the small pimple that had taken root above his right eyebrow, and the half-moon scar that traced the edge of his mouth.

"Were you serious?" she asked. "About being able to take me somewhere?"

"Sure, it's—"

"In Duncerton. And it's only if you let me pay for the gas."

His eyes slid down to the gas gauge, noting the needle that hovered above the halfway mark. Duncerton was only twenty minutes to the east, no more than a belch and a holler away.

"You don't have to give me money," he said.

"Yes, I do. I don't even know you, and you already picked me up in the middle of nowhere earlier, and then I sabotage you and jump into your car after I stupidly walk out in front of it . . ."

She fidgeted in her seat as she trailed off.

"I do," she said again in a hushed voice.

The road ended with a stop sign and they turned onto Grady Drive. They were on their way then, straight toward Duncerton. Straight toward Scotty.

What are you doing? Sarah asked herself, watching the trees pass in a blur outside her window. The answer, of course, was self-explanatory. Have a fight with the boyfriend? Run home to Mom. No love there? Just choose a friend and sprint to them. There was always an option. Always a back-up person.

So why Scotty? her inner voice challenged. *You've barely thought of him lately, let alone talked with him.*

It was easy enough to tell herself that she just needed someone neutral to vent to . . . but she knew it was a load of bull. There was no one else. Matt had wedged himself between her and her friends, slowly forcing them out of her life.

Come on, a little voice whispered, *did Matt really drive away all your friends?*

So maybe some of it had been her fault. She wasn't about to shoulder all the blame, but maybe she had started calling her friends a little less often after she and Matt started dating. It was a perfectly normal thing to do. Friends were always pushed to the side when a boyfriend or girlfriend entered the scene. Hell, it had happened to her too many times to count. So maybe it wasn't all Matt, but it was *because* of Matt, and wasn't that the same thing?

You're an expert at skimming the truth. You almost have yourself convinced.

She began to get angry at the voice—the voice that was making her feel like the criminal of the night.

Matt had scared the hell out of her; *that* was truth. Her mother had slapped her; *that* was truth.

And you caused none of it, the voice challenged . . . and she was uncertain if it was a statement or a question. She had engaged in conversations with herself for as long as she could remember, and now she was starting to wonder how normal it really was. When you had to defend yourself *against* yourself, maybe it was time to seek some help. Like her mother always said—

She pushed the thought away, not ready to think about her mother. She still couldn't believe what she had said. But it hadn't come out the way she had meant . . . it had just been . . .

Heat of the moment?

She bit her lip, denying a comparison between the fight with her mother and the fight with Matt. They were two different situations, two different motivations. She had gotten upset with her mother while defending herself; Matt had gotten upset at her because he was drunk. The whole ruination of the night could be traced back to the stupid party. Of course, he hadn't *made* them stop; only asked if they could. She was the one to say it was okay.

So . . . doesn't that make it your fault?

She wasn't about to accept that. What if she *had* said no? Wouldn't he have talked her into it anyway? And even though he was sober at that point, she wasn't about to make any speculations. Not after the way he had blazed at her, looking like he wanted to tenderize her with his fists. So shouldn't she be happy that everything had happened the way it did? By allowing them to stop at the party, she had inadvertently set into motion a series of events that had allowed her to finally see Matt for his true self. Otherwise they would have gone back to his place and maybe had sex, thus making it worse later on when she *had* found out about his dark side. So by that rationale, weren't the events of the night a good thing?

She shifted in her seat, her stomach a writhing pool waiting to explode. Thinking about it only made her ill, and the more she dwelled on it, the more messed up it became. Regardless, the bottom line remained the same: Matt shouldn't have asked if they could stop at the party. That was the point.

So you were pissed off at yourself for not having the gall to speak your mind and you took it out on him.

So maybe there was some truth in that as well, but it didn't change everything he had done. Especially that middle of the road shit. She honestly thought she had heard a car coming—

—and from his point of view you attacked him for no reason. And you wonder why he lashed out at you? You tell

your mom she's basically a slut and then wonder why she slaps you?

Newfound guilt settled inside her. Was she just a bitch that hurt everyone? She shivered and ran her hands down her arms, not wanting to think about it anymore.

"Are you cold?" he asked. "I can roll up my window if you want."

"I'm good," she replied faintly.

He smiled and returned his attention back to the road. At that moment she did feel like a bitch and felt horrible for everything she had put this poor kid through. Paying him for gas was a small and almost worthless gesture, but she had to do something.

"I really appreciate this," she said. "I know that probably doesn't mean much, but I wanted to say it."

"Most excitement I've had all year," he replied. "By the way, my name's Kevin."

"Sarah," said Sarah.

Her eyes lingered on him, and she wondered if he was young enough to still be in high school. He certainly didn't act it, but his features were almost boyish. Not in a bad sense, but more of a "nice-guy" way. He had to be a nice guy to be putting up with her.

She stared out the window, her lids opening and closing. All she wanted to do was shut off her brain. If she closed her eyes, the worst the kid might do was look down her shirt. She could live with that. The bumps in the road were too soothing.

She shut her eyes and let herself drift.

[5]

Kevin pulled the Camaro into the gas station and killed the engine. Sarah was curled up with her head propped against the window, her mouth opening and closing with each breath. If she wasn't asleep, she was doing an award-winning job of faking.

He climbed out and gently shut the door. She stirred in her seat and brushed a hand against her cheek. If someone had told him he was going to have a girl in his car that night, he would have laughed in their face. Mark was never going to believe any of it.

He took out his wallet and surveyed the damage. He wasn't about to take her money for gas, though there was no question he could use it.

"Why couldn't you be a credit card?" he muttered, flipping past his library card and taking out the twenty-dollar bill behind it. It was all that was left until next payday. He unscrewed the gas cap with a sigh, hoping there would at least be a couple bucks left for his wallet. He didn't want his library card to get lonely.

His hand wandered to his back pocket. The envelope was still there, a new future hidden away inside.

Possible future, he corrected himself. His other hand instinctively went to the silver cross hanging from his neck.

"You might actually have a future in writing, Mr. Reed," his teacher had told him after class. "Your stories are quite good."

It had been the final day of his junior year and all the other students had scattered with the bell. Mrs. Cauchniff had asked him to stay behind, and he knew he was busted for something. Busted for *what* he had no idea, but Mrs. Cauchniff wasn't one for casual conversation. She addressed all the students by their last names, and the rare times she did smile, it looked like she wanted to devour your soul.

"Thanks," he replied, too stunned to say much else. The entire year she had given him high marks on the assignments, but other than that, she had never singled him out in any real way. He just assumed she was as indifferent toward him as the other kids.

"You have a lot of raw talent," she said, folding her hands together on top of her desk. She was staring at him fiercely, and he wondered how a person could say something kind and yet still look cross. It was a bizarre combination.

"Yes, the talent is evident," she continued, "but your prose is sloppy. Your mechanics are a mess. Fortunately, those can be learned. If it wasn't for content, you would probably end up with a C in my class."

He knew he wasn't the best writer in the world, but he didn't feel he rated that. He *had* been writing since the age of twelve.

"There seems to be a central motif in your work, Mr. Reed, and I always find it interesting to see what people can do without realizing it. Do you follow?"

"I'm not sure."

"Callie always writes about animals in her stories. Crista uses lots of colors and sounds. Cara always references novels that she loves. Are you following me now?"

To the damn point, he thought with a nod.

"Your protagonists are always lost souls, searching for something that either seems impossible or is out of their reach. But your stories always make me smile at the end."

"Smile?"

"They always end on the same note. *Hope*. Regardless of how bad things are or what the characters have to endure, they always stick it out and never give up."

"I guess I never thought about it," he answered.

"Do you remember the first assignment you turned in, Mr. Reed? It was entitled *Moon Bridge*. The way you captured the son's emotions under the thumb of his abusive father . . . why, I think I almost wanted to cry when I read it. Have you written any more about that character?"

"No," he answered quickly.

She leaned back in her chair. "Did you know that I was once married, Mr. Reed?"

He shrugged. All the kids knew, and anybody that had her for a teacher could figure out why she was divorced. One could only imagine what it would be like to actually *live* with the woman. An hour a day was torture enough.

"I was married," she said, "and it was a terrible thing. Not for the reasons you might think, however. He was a teacher at my college, and I was one of his students. I was enthralled by him. There was, of course, an age difference to speak of, but who cared? I was in love. We were married and my parents and all my friends refused to come to the wedding. They all knew it was wrong, but I couldn't see it."

She lowered her head.

"It didn't take long for things to turn sour. I didn't fit in with his friends, and outside of literature, we found we had little in common. He turned mean and abusive. I suffered horrors with that man, and he never lifted more than his tongue at me. It's frightening what people can do with words. They are a powerful weapon in and of themselves. And after a while you start to believe those words, even if a small part of you deep down knows they are untrue. I was lucky. Even though I lived with him, I could do something about it. I moved out and removed myself from the situation. Not everyone can do that, I realize, and even I stayed around much longer than I should have. Do you know what finally did it for me?"

"What?" he asked.

She paused, waiting until he met her eyes.

"I was sitting on the steps of my porch feeling sorry for myself. I had no one at that time. I hadn't spoken with my parents, and I had fallen out of touch with my friends. This was in the span of five months, but it doesn't take long for the water to grow deep once you've made your island.

"I heard a noise and saw the neighbor lady leaving her house. This woman was in her eighties and had some . . . let's say mental confusion. Once a week, she would go for a walk and pull a dog leash behind her. Apparently, she didn't know or care that there was no dog attached.

"'My dear,' she asked, 'whatever is the matter?'

"I hadn't realized I had been weeping, and I wasn't in the habit of sharing my problems with people I hardly knew. In my younger years I had a rather loose and curt tongue.

"'Go away,' I told her. 'It's not your concern.'

"'It can't be that awful,' was her reply. 'Maybe this will help.'

"The woman reached into her purse and brought out a necklace. Dangling from the end was a silver cross the length of a paperclip.

"'My late husband Earl gave this to me,' she said. 'It was right after I had my miscarriage. He told me to trust in the Lord and wear it always. God can always make it better. It always made me so happy . . . maybe it will cheer you up as well.'

"Before I knew what had happened, she placed the necklace on the step and wandered away with a smile. I was too flabbergasted to speak. For this woman to give me this without another thought and then simply leave? I didn't know what to think! There I was, tears running down my cheeks, and suddenly, I felt *more* horrible than I had before. If a complete stranger could show me such an act of unconditional kindness, what kind of person was I to allow myself to live with someone like Aaron? A complete stranger was more benevolent than he, and I was purposely with him!"

She caught her breath then, realizing she had been speaking rapidly. A crooked smile formed on her lips.

"I know what the kids think of me. I know the things they say. Mrs. Crotch-sniff is by far the least original. I've never heard you say anything in particular, but I imagine you've thought it."

Kevin opened his mouth to speak, and she flapped a hand at him.

"Don't patronize me. It doesn't matter. But I will tell you two things that do. One, I have been at the bottom, and I know that it can get better. Believe me when I say I am not a bitter person because of what I had to endure. If you saw me in a relaxed moment, I might even remind you of a kindly grandmother. I am hard on my students because I want to be their teacher. I want them to *learn*. Whether or not they like me is immaterial. Do you understand?"

Kevin swallowed and cleared his throat. "And the second thing?"

"You are the most gifted student I have had the pleasure of working with. Don't throw that away. The world is a more interesting place with you in it, Mr. Reed."

She held out the silver cross.

"Kindness comes in all forms, and not always from people you know or like. I am not a religious person, but this was always a powerful symbol for me. It was a symbol of hope, and many nights I lay awake holding it, remembering the old woman that had taken the time to simply stop and speak with me. The last time it was around my neck was right before I married my second husband, Langley. I do not require it anymore, and I would very much like you to have it."

He tentatively reached out and lifted it from her hand.

"I would like to say that I hope you still have it when you make your mark on the world, but perhaps you will find another purpose for it before then."

He closed his fingers around the cross. She was looking at him with an almost benevolent smile, and he thought that was perhaps the scariest smile of all.

"Is that a true story, Mrs. Cauchniff?" he asked.

For just a moment, her eyes glistened. "Mr. Reed, you may *believe* what you like."

A door slammed and Kevin jumped at the sound. An old guy with thinning white hair had pulled into the pump beside him and was unscrewing the gas cap on a rusty pickup.

Lost time, he told himself. *You're way too young to be dabbling in that realm.*

Kevin dolefully marched inside the store and surrendered the twenty to the clerk. Sarah was still asleep when he returned, fidgeting and mumbling under her breath. Her hands brushed across her chest, batting at something that wasn't there. Kevin unclasped his necklace and paused to give it a final glance. It had never been off his neck since he had received it, and without hesitation he dropped it into her open purse. A small cry escaped her mouth; she looked like she was capable of bursting into tears even as she slept.

"*Good* dreams," he whispered.

Her eyelids fluttered as he started the engine.

• • •

—the window shattered and she let out a scream as he hissed at her through the broken glass, the kitchen knife gleaming between his teeth and cutting his upper lip as he pulled it out and jabbed it at her, shrieking, "I get what I want; didn't I tell you if you tried to leave me, I'd make you so sorry you'd never forget it? If I can't have you, no one else will—"

—and then he was on her with his hands ripping and tearing her clothes and driving the knife up inside—

• • •

"—get away!" Sarah screeched.

"What?" Kevin cried, jerking upright. The steering wheel bucked in his hands as the car slid into the gravel, and he swiftly maneuvered back onto the road. Sarah was looking frantically in all directions.

"What's wrong?" he asked. His voice had a hard edge to it that he didn't like, but she had startled the shit out of him.

"Matt," she rasped.

"Who?"

Movement in the road caught his eye, and he saw the animal a split second before it disappeared under the car with a small crunch. He slammed on the brakes and the Camaro came to a skidding, sliding stop. She threw open the car door and stumbled to the side of the road.

"Sarah?"

He got out and circled around the car. She was bent forward with her hands on her knees, pulling in slow, dragging breaths.

"Are you okay?" he asked in a shaky voice.

She nodded without looking up. "Yeah. I think so. I just . . . I need a minute."

"Yeah," he said. "Sure."

He moved to the rear of the car, gave her one last glance, and then peered down the road. *And what did we hit, anyway?*

He started toward the dark bundle. There was only the moonlight and the glow of his taillights to work with, but he could still make out the mangled shape of an animal. A dark pool of blood was forming around its head and soaking into the pavement.

"Bad luck," he whispered.

He re-approached the Camaro slowly and leaned against the fender, unsure of what to say. Sarah was sitting on the ground with her knees drawn up and caged in her arms.

"I didn't mean to shout," she said. "I . . . didn't know I was asleep."

"It's okay."

"No, it's *not* okay. I don't even know you, and here I am putting you through all *this*. I can't imagine what you're thinking right now."

Kevin said, "I'm thinking that I'm with a girl who has had a very difficult evening."

Her eyes darted to his. "And I'm thinking the only reason you're able to put up with me is because you're a serial killer."

It hung oddly in the air, and he realized their eyes were locked together.

"Or an escaped mental patient," he replied.

It slipped out unintentionally, and he cursed himself for the timing of his wit. To his surprise, she smiled.

"Or both," she said.

He relaxed as she turned away, unfazed by the exchange. Now they were okay with each other. He hoped.

"Where are we?" she asked.

"A few minutes outside of Duncerton."

She began to work herself upright, and he reached out and took her hand. Her gaze moved to the road behind them.

"It was a cat," he said.

"Is it dead?"

"Yeah. I wouldn't look if I were you. It's not pretty."

She settled back into the passenger seat. "You did the right thing, you know. Whether you meant to or not."

"What do you mean?"

"I know it sounds horrible, but you did the right thing by hitting it. I had a cousin who swerved out of the way to avoid a raccoon and lost control of the car. He hit a tree."

"Was he hurt badly?"

She stared at him, the dome light illuminating her face, which was pale and tear-streaked. "He died."

"Oh."

"At any given moment something bad can happen, completely out of the blue and unexpected. That's just the way it is, isn't it?"

"I suppose," he answered.

"Is it just me, or is the car sitting weird? This side seems lower than the other side."

Kevin stepped back to examine the car. "Shoot. The back tire is flat."

"Did that happen when we hit the cat?"

"Maybe. Or I might have picked up a nail or a piece of metal when the car went into the gravel. Feel free to stay inside the car. It'll just take a couple of minutes to fix."

"Okay."

She waited until he was gone, then flipped down the visor to see if she looked as bad as she felt. The eye shadow that had been applied earlier with surgical skill was mostly gone, along with all traces of her blush. She normally didn't wear the stupid junk, but Matt liked it when she "dolled" up. That was what he called it, anyway. She had even offered to change out of her tank top and jeans when he informed her they were going to the most expensive restaurant in town, but he had hurried them out the door, claiming they needed to be there by six to keep the reservation. Looking back now, she knew it was a form of punishment. Matt always hated the way she dressed and—in his mind—was undoubtedly trying to teach her a lesson. In Matt's world, clothes *did* make the man, and you dressed for success. For her, it was all about comfort. And it hadn't bothered her one bit when everyone in the restaurant had tossed glances her way as they were seated. She had been too enthralled with the place to care. She had never been inside—only heard people talk of it. It was the place where all the grown-ups converged to celebrate anniversaries and special occasions. She had even spotted one of her old high school teachers there with his family. Nothing had ever made her feel more adult than that moment, rubbing elbows with the elite of Centerview. And outside of a slightly overcooked steak, it had been wonderful. By then, Matt had gotten over his annoyance with her, undoubtedly because he had remembered he was on a mission to get laid after the meal.

She pushed the visor back into place and heard the kid moving items inside the trunk. Then, unmistakably: "Shit!"

She stepped out, cautioning herself about offering help. The last thing she wanted was a repeat of earlier that evening.

"What's wrong?" she asked.

"You don't happen to have a spare tire in your purse, do you?"

She peered into the trunk and noticed two things simultaneously: an unzipped duffel bag stuffed with clothing and what looked to be a spare tire.

"You were right," Kevin said. "Bad things happen for no reason."

She took a startled step backward and almost tripped over her feet. The kid wasn't looking at her, but she could see the malicious grin hardening on his face as his hand found the tire iron.

God, please no, she cried silently, trying to find the strength to run. All the energy drained from her legs.

"You're white as a sheet," he said, turning to face her. "Are you going to pass out?"

The last thing she knew he was reaching for her, and before everything went black, a single word slipped from her lips: *Scotty*.

TWO

He pulled the sheet to his chin and watched her out of the corner of his eye. She was propped up in the bed beside him, one hand holding her book firmly in place while the other hand endlessly twirled a strand of long, blonde hair. Her eyes were serious and focused behind her glasses, and every time she exhaled, her nostrils flared slightly. A small grin touched his lips.

"You know how much I hate this," she said, turning the page. "Don't you have anything better to do?"

"What am I doing?" he asked innocently.

"You're staring at me."

"You have a booger hanging."

She sighed and set the book on the nightstand. Then she carefully removed her glasses. "You asked for it."

She straddled him with a grin and started slapping his arms and chest. "You like that, punk? Huh? Do ya?"

"That all you got?" he asked with a hearty laugh. He bucked her sideways and attacked her armpits with his fingers. "You asked for it, *big* time!"

She dissolved into laughter. "You gotta stop! Mercy!"

"You promise you give up?"

"Yes!"

He stopped tickling but didn't remove his hands. It was only when he was feeling really feisty that he took it to the next level.

And he was feeling feisty.

"I'm gonna get 'em," he cackled.

She was laughing so hard she was crying. "Oh, please, *please* . . ."

He grabbed her foot and began to tickle. Her hands pounded into his back. "I'm begging you! I'm going to pee my pants!"

He released her and rolled off the bed in the event of a counterstrike. Her laughs were deep hitches inside her throat as she wiped away tears from her eyes.

"Don't mess with the best," he said, opening the window to cool off and give her a moment to compose herself. Once she started giggling, it sometimes took her forever to wind down. And he could easily get her going again; all he had to do was wiggle his fingers in her direction and she would start laughing. It was pretty amazing.

"Jerk," she said, coming over and poking his stomach. "And to think I've been feeling bad for you because you're so freaked out about flying tomorrow."

"Me? Freaked out? Never. I'm looking forward to spending three hours in a metal coffin that's suspended thirty thousand feet above the ground."

She pinched his waist. "Now, darling, what are we trying to remember?"

"That to take a flight is to unnecessarily risk your life—"

"Try again."

He relented. "Hundreds of pilots and flight attendants fly every day and they don't die. Usually."

"That's my trooper," she said, giving him a squeeze.

"We're gonna crash!" he cried, grabbing her hand and pulling her back to the bed. She gave an audible *oof!* as they fell onto the mattress and he landed on top of her.

"I think you just collapsed my stomach," she said with a groan.

"Sorry, my love."

He rolled to his side of the bed, and she hit him with her pillow before repositioning it behind her. "This isn't over. Mark my words, buddy."

"I'll give you a rematch anytime, anywhere. *If* we survive the death plane and escape death—"

"Shhh. Did you hear that?" She leaned forward and stared into the bedroom door. "I thought I just heard a noise.

It sounded like it was right outside our door." She lowered her voice. "I think he's out there, listening to us."

"I don't hear anything. You're being paranoid."

She settled back with a frown. "How much longer is he going to stay with us again?"

"I don't know. Not long. What can I do? He is my brother."

"I'm sorry if this sounds horrible," she said, "but sometimes he gives me the creeps. And I never know what to say to him."

"Dad's death really screwed him up. He never used to be like this. I'm surprised you don't hear him in the middle of the night."

"Hear him?"

He gestured toward the wall. "The poor kid barely sleeps, and when he does, it usually ends in nightmares. He tosses and turns and sometimes cries out."

"I had no idea. Have you asked him about it?"

"I brought it up once or twice, but he doesn't seem interested in talking. He'll work it out eventually." He leaned over and pecked her on the cheek. "Thanks for being such a peach about everything."

She reached toward the ceiling in a long stretch. He watched her breasts gently rise and fall beneath her nightgown. She shot him a glance and raised her eyebrows.

"And what's on *your* mind, mister?"

"Oh, a couple little things."

"*Little*?" she asked sharply.

"Just my size," he whispered, sliding a hand up her gown.

There was a knock on the bedroom door. "Wade?"

"Hold on," Wade said, leaping from the bed as the door began to open. He caught it halfway and pushed his brother back out into the hallway. "Scotty, your timing couldn't be worse."

"Sorry. I'm heading out in a couple minutes. I probably won't see you in the morning before you leave for your trip."

"Just don't burn the place down when we're gone. The phone numbers for where we're staying are on the table in case of an emergency. The one at the top is for Stephanie's brother."

Scott nodded and pushed his bangs away from his eyes.

"Jeez, kid," Wade said, "get a haircut when we're gone, will ya? At least it's not long in the back. Mom would have a fit if she saw you these days."

"Sure. Hey, I really appreciate you letting me crash here. As soon as I get things patched up with my roommate, I'll be out of your hair. No fuss, no muss."

Wade gave him a weary smile and lowered his voice. "Get out of here so I can have some alone time with your sister-in-law."

"Okay," Scott said, making no motion to leave. He peeked into the bedroom as the door closed, catching a glimpse of Stephanie with her arms crossed protectively over her chest. She was almost disgustingly perfect in her looks. Blonde hair, blue eyes, and just a hint of freckles scattered across her nose. His brother got all the breaks.

Scott returned to the guest bedroom, pulled on his jacket, and did a quick inventory of the pockets. The only thing missing was his glasses, but those were still being held hostage at the old place. It was no big loss. Things were only fuzzy and distorted at a distance, but up close, everything was fine and dandy. And that was all that really mattered. Anything that wasn't directly in your face wasn't worth the bother.

He took a final look around and glanced at the clock. He was going to be late if he didn't get moving. He was always late.

"Ohhh!"

The cry was from Wade's room. Scott inched into the hallway with his head raised. Stephanie cried out again from behind the door as the bed came to life, creaking and groaning in protest. Scott pressed his ear against the door and touched the knob. There was another cry from her—this time sharp and loud. It sounded like Wade was hurting her. The headboard slammed against the wall as the panting and moaning began to escalate. His brother was grunting now, sounding like a tiny, angry dog. Stephanie moaned endlessly.

"Oh, Wade," she sang. "Wade . . ."

Scott withdrew from the door. It could have been him in there; that much was obvious from the way Stephanie acted around the house. The way she "accidentally" forgot to close the bathroom door when she dressed in the mornings. How she constantly bent forward while wearing low cut blouses. How her legs were always spread whenever she sat in a skirt. She was the worst kind of tease—flaunting her shit at every opportunity. He didn't understand how Wade couldn't see it. Maybe when they returned from their trip, Scott would open his brother's eyes. Make him see. It was the least he could do to repay him.

He found his shoes by the front door and pulled them on. The laces were frayed and thin and almost tattered beyond use, just like everything else in his life. He saw Stephanie's purse on the floor and dug out her wallet. There was a handful of bills inside, and he carefully pocketed a ten and two fives. Just a loan, that was all. Enough to get some new shoelaces. Maybe some cigarettes. Taking a bit of money didn't make him a bad guy. There were way worse people than him in the world. Way worse *things* in the world.

He peered out the window into the darkness. The corner streetlight was out, and he told himself it was coincidence, nothing more.

"Way worse things," he said in a whisper.

He lingered a moment longer before crossing through the kitchen and slipping out the back door into the waiting night.

[6]

Someone was calling her name.

Sarah tried to open her eyes, but it felt as if tiny weights had been attached to the lids. When she tried to lift her head there was an explosion of pain. She lashed out with her tongue, trying to form some sort of cry. The voice called on her again, soft and distant and barely recognizable.

Am I dead?

Everything felt wrong. Tiny rocks were biting her arms and her legs felt scrunched and twisted.

Wake up! her inner voice shouted.

Her eyes snapped open. The darkness lingered, but something was in it. Not something—*someone.*

"Sarah?"

His name is Kevin . . .

This time she did lift her head, and another spike of pain reeled across her forehead. She was lying on the ground. Her purse was still latched around her shoulder, but most of its contents had spilled onto the pavement. Kevin was on one knee beside her.

"What happened?" she asked.

"You fainted," he said hoarsely. "Holy crap, please don't do that again."

She worked herself upright. "Fainted?"

"I was looking at the flat spare tire and said something dumb like, 'You don't have a spare, do you?' The next thing I knew, you were falling forward."

She lightly touched her forehead and found a small mound above her left eye the size of a gumball.

"The spare in the trunk is *flat*?" she asked.

He pushed out an angry sigh. "I try to check it every few months to make sure it still has air, but I kind of spaced it off. Stupid me."

"You have clothes in the trunk," she said, shaking her head. "What did . . . I . . . I thought . . ."

Clothes of his victims? she scolded herself. *Sarah, is that really what you thought?*

"It's just a bag with some of my stuff."

"Stuff?"

"Let me guess . . ." He arched his eyebrows. "Psycho killer, right?"

She began shoving the fallen items back into her purse. "I'm sorry. I'm *so* sorry."

"Go slowly," he told her. "The weight of that bruise alone is going to be enough to throw you off balance for the next few days."

"How can you keep this up?" she asked miserably. "First I ruin your night, then I ruin your car . . . even *I* hate me right now."

He gave her a sympathetic smile as he stood. "First of all, the only thing I'd be doing right now is sitting at home, bored. Secondly, I don't think getting a flat is considered *ruining* a car, especially when you had nothing to do with it. I should feel bad for giving you that welt."

She touched her forehead again. *Did I fall on my face?* she thought stupidly. *I'm sure that looked cool.*

"It really wasn't that bad," he said, reading her thoughts. "I managed to catch most of you. At the last minute your head rolled forward and banged my knee. Sorry."

"Don't be sorry," she said with a gasp. "God, you're the last person here who needs to apologize."

"Well . . ." He offered a small shrug. "The good news is there's a gas station about a mile back. I can get some tire gunk there."

"Some what?"

"It's an aerosol can that inflates the tire with a paste that plugs the hole. It's not a permanent fix, but it should get us where we're going." He looked over his shoulder. "It shouldn't take too long to walk there. Feel free to wait here and stay comfortable inside the car."

"No," she replied quickly, picking herself up from the ground. The last thing she wanted was to be left alone again. "I'll come with you."

"Are you sure?"

She thought of Matt. Was he still stranded by the side of the road, waiting for her to come back? Maybe he had gotten her car started and was over at her house right now with her mother, telling her what a wretch her daughter was.

Or maybe—just maybe—he's driving all over town and looking for you. And what do you think is going to happen when he finds you?

"Yeah," she nodded. "I'd rather walk than sit."

She waited while Kevin rolled up the windows, pondering the odds of being stranded twice in one night, and more importantly, what cosmic forces were at work, and why had they picked her birthday to reveal themselves.

[7]

Scott moved hastily across the lawn of the church, wondering if it was blasphemous to walk on God's green grass. But it was the quickest route to the hotel, and that was all that mattered. When he stood before the Big Guy living in the clouds, he would worry about discussing the details of how he had lived his life. And that was such a reach into the future that he couldn't grasp it. Some scientist would surely come up with some sort of immortality process before he was old enough to worry about it, or at least figure out how to increase the life span of a person two or three hundred years. All kinds of people were working on stuff like that because no one wanted to die. Even somewhere in the Bible it said that dying was a mistake . . . something about the meek inheriting the earth? Some bible-slinging neighbors had stopped by his parents' house once and informed them of it. And they couldn't lie. It was a sin for them to lie.

"Forgive me because I sinned," he said. He thought of doing that thing where you touched your forehead, stomach, and both shoulders . . . what Aunt Margaret did every time she saw an ambulance or heard sirens wailing in the distance. He didn't understand it or care about it. He and God each minded their own business. It was safer that way.

He crossed by the park and turned his head at the swings rattling in the wind. The empty playground equipment looked like dark hulking monsters, waiting to eat up small children. The surrounding houses were all large and sleek, the lawns trimmed and immaculate. Everything on the street was in order; the only thing that didn't belong there was him. And all at once, it angered him to think of the people inside, slumbering away with no worries and no open windows. They were better than the things that came out at night; the things that walked the streets.

But they were cowards.

Their windows were locked, their curtains shut, but he could sense them watching. That was what they did: peeked out at the world from the inside, spying on their cars and yards.

He pulled a quarter from his pocket. The car beside him was crimson red and looked expensive.

"Are you watching me?" he whispered, running the coin across the car door. A jagged white line appeared in the paint. His eyes jumped from house to house, daring someone to come forward; to forgo the police and face him like a man. Right versus wrong; rich versus poor; good versus evil. Whatever you wanted to call it.

He waited a moment longer before wiping a shaky hand across his mouth and trekking on. The windows became square eyes, boring into him as he walked. The sense of being watched was very real—the whisper of a presence tickling the hairs on the back of his neck. Not from someone inside a house, but something else. Something that had been with him since the death of his dad.

"He's dead," Scott said with quiet firmness, "and it wasn't my fault."

A branch snapped behind him and unseen fingers tugged at his face, trying to turn his head. His hand slid into his pocket and touched the pocketknife inside. There was no reason to turn because nothing was there. Ghosts weren't real; his dad was dead; everything he felt and heard was all in his mind—

"Liar!"

He spun around, a terrified wail escaping his mouth. No one was behind him. He scanned both sides of the street and even stupidly looked toward the sky. The stars looked down on him like tiny glittering eyes. He gripped the knife, but the gesture felt stupid and pointless; the blade was barely two inches long.

"No one," he croaked.

He stood without breathing, trying to focus his eyes between the car he had scratched and the house behind it. There was a dark shape beside the wooden fence, and he told himself it was only a shrub or a bush . . . no matter how much it looked like a person crouching and watching.

He hurried down the road on trembling legs, not daring to look back over his shoulder.

[8]

Sarah Melissa Cate, she told herself for the umpteenth time, *you have absolutely no class.*

She and Kevin were halfway back to the Camaro, but her mind was still stuck at the gas station. Everything had gone downhill after she asked if he wanted some plastic water. He had given her a blank stare and tilted his head to one side.

Bottled water, she told him. *You know . . . because it's in a plastic bottle?*

Very clever, he had said with a smile . . . and she hadn't known if he was making fun of her or not. But that hadn't been the worst. The worst was when she told him she needed to use the "grunt" room.

The what? he asked with a laugh.

It was an expression Matt used freely, and one that apparently had incorporated itself into her daily vocabulary without her realizing it. Matt wasn't around and he was still ruining everything.

You don't need to explain that one, Kevin had told her.

She wanted to tell him she just needed to go pee—she didn't need to *grunt* about anything—but decided not to embarrass herself more by trying to fumble out an explanation. Hopefully the fact that she had done her business in about two seconds before hurrying back out was explanation enough. And then at the counter she had knocked over a display of aspirin with her elbow while fumbling for her money. Oh, it had been glorious.

"You really didn't have to pay for my stuff," Kevin said, breaking apart her thoughts.

"Please. It was the *least* I could do."

"So what's in Duncerton?" he asked. He was chewing on a candy bar and a small piece of chocolate was smeared across his upper lip. She was about to mention it when he wiped his hand across his mouth, removing all evidence.

"My friend J.D. lives there," she said and then laughed. "I mean, Scotty."

"Is J.D. his last name or something?"

She smiled and took a drink of water. He was watching her closely and she didn't know why.

"His name is Scotty. I used to call him J.D. sometimes. For James Dean. The actor."

"James Dean," Kevin repeated thoughtfully. "He's dead now . . . right?"

"Yeah."

"*East of Eden,*" Kevin said, snapping his fingers. "That was one of his movies."

She found herself nodding as a welt of excitement jumped inside her. She was more than willing to talk about something she loved to keep her mind off everything else.

"He was also in *Rebel Without a Cause* and *Giant*," she informed him.

"I remember watching *East of Eden* years ago. I liked the book so much that I wanted to see the movie. John Steinbeck, you know."

She didn't, but nodded politely.

"So why him?" Kevin asked.

"Huh?"

"Why do you call him J.D.?"

She laughed. "It's kind of an inside joke. Every time we'd watch a James Dean movie, Scotty would imitate him for weeks afterward. Dumb stuff like slicking back his hair or sulking around while trying to look morose and cool."

"So you're a big fan of his? James Dean, not your friend, I mean."

"Ask me anything."

"Uh . . . when was he born?"

"February eighth, nineteen thirty-one," she said with a frown. "Can't you think of anything harder?"

He gave an apologetic shrug.

"Scotty and I grew up together. He only lived a few blocks away from us and our parents were friends from before we were born. It was in high school that we discovered

James Dean." She looked at him. "You sure you want to hear this?"

"Absolutely."

"It was a weekend night and we were at my house. I, of course, had secured the remote control, as one of my favorite things to do is channel zip—"

"Channel zip?"

"You know, zip through the channels."

"I don't really watch much television," he confided.

"God, I *live* by it," she exclaimed, and then felt stupid when he gave her a look she couldn't decipher.

"Anyway," she said quickly to pass the moment, "we came across an old movie with two guys knife fighting, and we were immediately hooked. Turns out it wasn't a movie but a documentary about this guy named James Dean from the fifties."

She paused to take a sip of water and told herself she was talking too much. But he didn't seem bothered by it and it was helping to pass the time.

"When it was over, we went down to the video store and found *East of Eden*. We went back home and watched it, and after Scotty left, I watched it again. I think I watched it a total of four times before finally returning it to the store."

"Wow," he said. "You're obsessed."

She looked at him with a start, but when she saw the grin on his face she returned it with ease.

"Yeah, maybe," she agreed. "I fell in love that weekend."

"With James Dean or Scotty?"

"James Dean," she answered quickly. "Scotty and I are just friends."

She cleared her throat and took a gulp of water. A car drove past, leaving behind a blast of music and taillights.

"How about you?" she asked. "Who's your hero?"

He opened his mouth and closed it. She felt the urge to playfully punch him in the shoulder, but resisted.

"Come on," she coaxed. "You have to do some of the talking here, or I'm going to run out of water before I run out of mouth—"

"Stephen Matheson."

"Matheson," she said, wrinkling her nose. "Isn't he the guy who writes all those horror books?"

"Pretty much."

"And when was *he* born?"

"March twentieth, nineteen forty-eight at eleven forty-three in the p.m. Born Stephen Michael Matheson, son of Kenneth and Alice—"

"I get the point," she said with a laugh, and this time did whap him on the shoulder. The can of tire gunk under his arm dropped to the ground and clattered down the road. He chased it down and scooped it up.

"Sorry," she said with a grin.

"No harm, no foul."

"Do you read a lot?"

"Reading and writing are sort of a hobby."

"You're a writer?" she asked. "Like journalism?"

"Not really, no." He began fumbling with the empty water bottle in his hands. "I've written a bunch of stories."

"Stephen Matheson-like stories?"

"Sometimes."

She stuck out her tongue. "Gross."

He smiled. "Not a noble trade, eh?"

"No," she answered with a start. "No, I'm not trying to say it's not a good thing . . ." She fought down the urge to bite off her tongue.

"I'm only giving you a hard time," he said, leaning into her. "Besides, I'm not dangerous yet. I haven't reached the status of professional or anything. That's the difference between a writer and an author, you know: an author gets *paid*."

"So what do you do with these stories?"

"I send them to magazines."

He was wringing the empty bottle of water now, and she was worried she was annoying him with the questions. But he was grinning like a little boy in a toy store.

"Try to get published," he continued. "Someday have a novel published."

Suddenly it dawned on her—he wasn't getting angry, he was getting excited. He was talking about something he loved. A smile sprang to her lips, and he closed his mouth with a snap.

"I'm babbling," he said, "aren't I?"

"No. Not at all. Have you had anything published?"

"One of my stories was accepted last month, actually. But just for a small, online publication. It really isn't a big deal. I didn't get paid for it or anything."

"And I can go online and see it?" she asked, fascinated.

"Eventually. It'll still be a couple months before it's on the site."

"Then I might just have to give you my e-mail so you can let me know when it's there. Then I can tell all my friends that I know a published writer."

"Sure."

They continued on in silence, and she breathed a small sigh of relief when they reached the Camaro. A small headache was pulsating behind her eyes, and her feet were screaming bloody murder.

"It should only take a few minutes to fix," he told her, unlocking the passenger side door.

"Thanks."

She collapsed into the seat and glanced at her watch. The last time she had checked it was around nine, and it was now a little after eleven.

Two hours ago? she thought in disbelief.

She marveled again about the events of the evening. She could hear Kevin moving around, fixing the tire, and it occurred to her that this guy—this random *kid*—had probably done more for her in one night than Matt had done for her in their whole relationship. At the end of the day, she didn't need to be wined and dined—she just needed someone to say "bless you" when she sneezed. Someone who would be there for her. Someone she could count on. Unlike last Saturday, when she had planned a special home-cooked meal for her and Matt. Her mother and Kirby were out for the night, and she had spent the whole day cleaning and preparing. When it came time to make the muffins, she realized there was no milk for the batter, and she had called Matt and asked him to pick some up and run it over. Somehow, he had talked his way out of it: the grocery store was too far out of the way; he hadn't showered yet; he was in the middle of a video game and couldn't quit . . . something. It was *always* something. He couldn't even put forth a tiny bit of effort for the special night she had planned. No, the only nice thing she could honestly remember in three months was earlier that night at the restaurant.

And you're tongue wrestling with Matt and taking advantage of Kevin, she told herself. *That makes sense.*

That was the problem, she suddenly decided: she always made friends easily enough—it was the romances she had problems with. She and Kevin would probably be chums for life after they got through this night.

"All gunked and good," Kevin said, climbing inside. "Just point your finger in the right direction and we'll be off and running."

She tried a smile and it fell flat. Scotty was no more than a few miles away, but it was anxiety she was feeling, not relief. It had been months since she had seen or talked to him, but they were friends of the strongest caliber. And old friends *could* go long spurts without speaking. You could always count on them, especially in a bind. That was the way it was supposed to work, but a small part of her wondered if she shouldn't just go back home. Maybe Scotty didn't want to see her.

Come on, Sarah, her inner voice scoffed, *do we have to play truth and fact again already?*

The fact was, in some strange sort of tiny, weird little way, a small part of her didn't want to find Scotty. She didn't know if it was crazy or pathetic, but the idea of separating from Kevin was sort of bumming her out.

So what do you want to do? Make this kid drive you around all night? Sure, he's been great for your morale, but he's probably as fed up with you as everyone else.

"Sarah?"

"Do you know where Creston Street is?" she asked.

"On our way," he said with a smile.

He dropped the car into gear and Sarah thought to herself: *You better be home, Scotty.*

[9]

Sarah knocked again, the ring on her finger making a small metallic click against the metal door. There was no doubt in her mind this was the right trailer; Scotty always called home the "yellow bus" and there was only one trailer in the entire park painted that color.

She cupped a hand over her eyes and tried to peer through the waved glass in the door. She was certain there had been a noise inside, and when the door jerked open, she skittered backward. A pixie-sized guy with flushed cheeks stepped out wearing boxer briefs and no shirt. His lower lip bulged with chew, and it smelled like he hadn't showered in weeks.

"Is Scotty home?" she asked timidly.

"Nope."

"Do you know when he'll be back?"

"When he starts payin half the rent," the guy answered, cleaning his belly button with his finger. "You a girlfriend or somethin?"

"Just a friend."

"Friend, huh? I never seen you before."

Sarah shrank back another step. "Do you know where he went?"

"Brother's house or somethin. If you see him, tell him his crap's gonna be on the street soon. You can also tell him he's gonna pay me for the dent he put in my car, and he still owes me for half of the water damage to the kitchen floor. You tell him that."

"Sure," Sarah said, moving away. "Sorry to bother you."

"You can bother me anytime," he called after her. "Sure you don't want to come inside and have a drink? Maybe we can figure out a way for you to help settle his debt. Ha!"

She shot him a glare as she climbed back into the Camaro.

"No luck?" Kevin asked.

"No. And why do people have to be so shitty?"

Kevin looked out her window as the trailer's door slammed shut. "Human nature and low self-esteem are usually the cause. Sometimes it can feel like the world is overrun with assholes. Do what I do. Instead of focusing on all the horrible people you interacted with today, focus on all the happy people."

"Today is not a good example," she said with a sigh.

"I just feel sorry for them."

She looked up. "Sorry?"

"Being an asshole is learned behavior. Trust me on this. What do you think that guy's old man is like? Probably kicked him down all his life until he was old enough to crawl away and start a shitty existence of his own."

"Yeah, maybe."

"Or look at it this way. If everyone in the world was nice, it wouldn't be a very interesting place to live in then, would it? And all the writers of the world would be silenced, because they'd have no one to pen their prose about. Then I'd have way too much free time and probably end up joining the asshole brigade myself."

She felt a small smile tug at her lips in spite of herself. "How is it that you always seem to know what to say?"

"I guess you just always ask the right questions."

Oh, please! she shouted at herself as they looked at each other. *Casual flirting or whatever you're doing is the last thing you need to be engaged in.*

"So I'm assuming that wasn't your friend?" Kevin asked.

"No," she replied. "Scotty . . . well . . ."

Just ask him to take you back home, she told herself. *Enough is enough. You're fighting a stupid battle. Your mother is probably worried sick, and Matt has probably called the police, thinking you've been raped and murdered.*

Kevin was still watching her with a queer smile. She tried to read his face and couldn't. She didn't know what to do.

Put yourself in his shoes. You force your way into his car, ask him to take you to another freakin town, and then say, "My mistake; take me back home"? No, she couldn't do that. She would have to play it out. She didn't have the courage to ask him to take her back to Centerview, which was stupid because he was going that way anyway. They lived in the same damn town.

"Um . . ." She bit her lip. "He's not at home, but I'm pretty sure I know how to find him."

"I am at your humble mercy," Kevin said somberly.

That's just not even funny, she thought, hiding a smile as he started the car.

[10]

Scott stepped into the lobby of the Night Owl Hotel and winked at the girl sitting behind the counter. She was a cute little thing with black hair and milky white skin. Her nametag read MANDY.

"May I help you, sir?" she asked.

"You can," he answered, fishing a mint out of the bowl on the counter. His gaze lingered on her chest as he popped the mint into his mouth and slowly began to suck.

"And *how* may I help you?" she asked.

"I am meeting my girlfriend here," he announced, raising his voice. "We will have sex here. Tonight!"

The girl smiled, exposing two crooked eyeteeth that resembled fangs. "Sounds intriguing. Do you need a room?"

He slapped a hand on the counter. "Only the best for me and my girl. What's the rate for your fanciest room?"

"That would be the honeymoon suite at the low price of two hundred and fifty dollars a night."

"Well, *nuts*. That's just a tad out of my price range. What's the cheapest room you have?"

"Sir, we do not have cheap rooms. We have *inexpensive* rooms."

Scott nodded as he popped another mint into his mouth. "And those cost how much?"

"Just under a hundred."

He motioned to the office behind her. "How much for the back room?"

"How long do you need it for?"

He considered. "Fifteen minutes?"

"I think we can manage that."

He grinned as he climbed over the counter. "I love the treatment here," he said, grabbing her by the waist and pulling her close.

"Get in here," she hissed.

They fell into the back room, and he somehow managed to shut the door with his foot.

[11]

Kevin parked next to a pickup with a bumper sticker that read *I never met a beer I didn't like*. The name of the bar was Billie's, and he made a mental note and filed it away. It was all going into the book.

It was the only rational explanation he could buy into for putting himself through the events of the night, and his fingers were itching to get it down on paper. The last few weeks of his mental constipation were about to be flushed away in one swoop. This was his next big project. Of course, the names and places would be changed to protect the innocent . . . and to protect himself against lawsuits.

"I'm so sorry," Sarah stammered. "I was sure I could find it again."

It had taken twenty minutes of driving in circles before she had confessed she had only been to the house once. And that had been in the daytime.

"It'll be in the phone book," Kevin said, knowing it probably wouldn't. Not with the way her luck was going. "I still can't believe I misplaced my cell phone last week. I'm hoping it will eventually turn up."

It was a white lie, but it wasn't like he was going to tell her that his father could barely afford the regular phone bill each month, let alone things like cell phones and internet. Now that school was out, he pretty much had zero access to e-mail or the internet.

He watched as she dug through her purse before his gaze inadvertently wandered to her breasts. They were small but almost perfect. He couldn't feel *that* guilty about groping her with his eyes—he was a guy, after all. Also, he was probably just being used and would never see her again after tonight. The funny thing was that it didn't really matter. Just being there with her was enough. The sound of her voice, the scent of her perfume—

Corny pathetic, he told himself. *Try putting that into a story and see how fast it gets laughed into the rejection pile.*

"Just one more sec," she said, pulling a small wallet from her purse.

He wondered if she was attracted to him at all. There had been a couple of times when she had tossed coy little smiles his way, but who could tell? Maybe she thought nothing of him. Or maybe tomorrow she would call and invite him over. He could already visualize it. A giant poster of James Dean would greet them as the front door opened.

Come inside, she would say. *Do you want something to drink?*

He would tell her no, but she would go into the kitchen anyway to be a good host. He would walk around her living room, smiling at everything he saw, and in the corner he would find a bookshelf with a dozen books by Stephen Matheson.

He's such a great writer, she would say, coming out from the kitchen with two drinks in her hands. But instead of offering him one, she would set both of them down.

You're going to be a great writer, she would tell him sternly.

He would laugh and shake his head.

I know you're going to make your mark on this world. Her hands would slide around the back of his neck, soft but firm. *Look me in the eyes and tell me you believe that.*

And before he could answer, she would lean into him and press her lips against his. Their tongues would touch, drifting inside each other's mouth, probing and exploring. And with a smile, she would pull back and say:

"Kevin, I hate to have to ask you this . . ."

He jerked up in the car seat. Little drops of sweat prickled his palms. She was talking to him. "Huh?" he managed to say.

She was still digging inside her purse. He wiped his sweaty hands on his jeans one at a time, telling himself she didn't notice.

"Don't hate me," she began.

"Yeah?" he asked cautiously.

She released a long sigh. "Sarah, you have to be in the lead for the 'Loser of the Year' award."

"What is it?"

"Do you have . . . fifty cents I can borrow?"

He blinked at her.

"I'm so sorry," she sputtered, "but I swear I had some change in here from the gas station, and instead of just getting the address from the phone book, I thought I would call to make sure Scotty's actually at his brother's house before dragging you anywhere else . . ."

Her hands moved through the air, going everywhere and nowhere.

"Can you do something for me?" he asked.

"Yes, of course. Anything."

He motioned to the car radio. "Look at the time."

"The time?" She looked at the clock on the radio. It read 11:35. "I know. It's getting *so* late—"

"I'm going to let you in on a secret," he said. "Every day, I try to do at least one nice thing for someone. It's a promise I made to myself a long time ago, and I stick to it. Always. Earlier I gave you a ride back into town when your car broke down, and then I drove you here to find your friend. That's *two* things."

He emphasized the point by holding up two fingers.

"And that's fine," he went on, "because sometimes if I'm feeling really good, I *let* myself do two nice things for someone in one day. It's still before midnight, so we're still legit for today's quota. But two is the absolute limit in one day."

Sarah studied him carefully, trying to decide if she was being put on.

"However," he said, "since it's technically almost Sunday, we can *pretend* it's the next day, and I can do one more nice thing for you. But this is it until Monday. We might find a small child trapped inside a burning building or something, so I gotta save the other 'good deed' for them."

He pulled open the ashtray. The inside was filled with coins, and he picked out two quarters and handed them over. She looked at them in her hand, unable to speak. All of her life had been spent in a meticulously structured world that was filled with people who were carefully selected for their individual traits. People who—she believed—inspired and amazed her. In one night that world had been rendered worthless, because no one in it had come close to how he had affected her in only a few hours.

"Would you like me to kiss you?" he asked.

"What?"

He smiled. "Would you like me to go with you? To the phone?"

Get a grip! she shouted at herself. *You don't even know what you're thinking anymore.*

"I'm good," she said, opening the car door. "Thanks."

She took in a sharp breath and started toward the pay phone in the corner of the lot. *What are you going to do about all this?*

She didn't know. All she knew was that the way he talked fascinated her. The way he made her feel . . .

But what does it mean?

She told herself it meant nothing. She was being stupid and reading into things. Hell, she didn't even know how old he was. Eighteen? Nineteen? She had never considered dating anyone younger than herself. He was just a kid.

"Focus," she told herself. Scotty was her first concern; everything else was for later.

She slowed as she neared the phone and saw that the directory had been ripped away. Not that it made a difference, because some idiot had jammed a piece of metal into the coin slot. It looked like the tab to a beer can.

"Perfect," she mumbled.

Something touched her shoulder and she spun, losing both quarters from her hand.

"Easy there, girlie," said the guy standing behind her. His jet-black hair was pulled into a man bun, and the cigarette between his lips moved up and down as he spoke. "Didn't mean to scare you out of your panties. Unless you wanted to be scared out of them, that is."

He grinned as she gave him a wary smile. "I'm good, thanks."

"I remember you. You were here last week."

"No," she said, kneeling down and finding one of the quarters by her feet. The other quarter was nowhere in sight.

"For someone who don't remember me, you sure remember that I love a girl on her knees."

She felt her pulse quicken and pushed in the front of her tank top, which had puffed open. She spotted the other quarter, and when she reached for it, the guy stomped on it with his foot.

"Is there a problem here?"

A shaky sigh escaped her mouth as she saw Kevin. The guy stepped back and held up his hands. "Just trying to help, bro. No problem here."

"We appreciate it," Kevin said.

The guy scooped up the other quarter and held it out to Sarah. When she didn't take it right away, he gave a coarse laugh.

"Take it," he said. "It's not gonna bite."

She tried to pluck it from his palm, but his hand closed around hers, turning it into a handshake. "See. We can be friends—"

Kevin's hand shot out and locked around the guy's wrist. The motion was so quick Sarah barely saw it happen.

"People lose wandering hands," Kevin said evenly.

Everything went into slow motion. It looked like two people arm wrestling without a table.

Kevin, what are you thinking? she wanted to cry . . . but it was the guy who was turning red and holding his breath.

Kevin's face was tight and serious, a small vein in his forehead bulging out. The guy gave a shout and the cigarette fell from his mouth.

"Okay," she said, grabbing Kevin by the arm. "Kevin, *stop*!"

Kevin released his grip and the guy lurched away so forcefully he almost fell backward.

"You better hope we don't meet again," the guy huffed, hurrying off in the other direction. Kevin stared at him until he was around the corner and out of sight.

"Kevin?"

His eyes had a distant, glazed look, and she prayed to God he wasn't going to go psycho on her like Matt had.

"Are you okay?" she asked.

He blinked and looked at her. "I'm fine. Are *you* okay?"

"Yeah," she said with a nod, but her head was spinning. "Just give me a minute."

She sat on a concrete block next to a pile of cigarette butts. The excitement was quickly fading, but she was still finding it difficult to catch her breath. She slipped a glance at Kevin and saw he was looking around the parking lot, almost surveying it. He was watching out for her. Making sure nothing else was coming her way, whether it was human or a natural catastrophe. She knew plenty of "tough guy" types, but they always were cocky and quick to show off. This guy was a writer. They were supposed to be nerdy and wimpy. She could only wonder what would have happened if the other guy hadn't stopped. She had never been fought over before and a small part of her was excited by the thought.

That's really dumb, Sarah. You write off Matt for being aggressive but then approve of Kevin doing it?

But it wasn't the same thing. Matt was aggressive toward her; Kevin was merely protecting her.

Or trying to impress you. Has it crossed your mind that this guy is doing and saying exactly what he knows will impress a distraught and emotional girl? Why else would he still be here helping you? He wants to get laid, just like all the others.

"Why did you do that, Kevin?"

"Was it wrong?"

She shook her head. "No."

"I guess . . . I didn't think you wanted him touching you."

There was a hint of something in his words that she couldn't read, and she stared at him curiously.

"Kevin, why are you doing all of this?"

"All of what?" he asked quietly.

She waved her hands in the air. "*This.* Driving me around, almost getting into fights because of me . . . I mean . . . I do have a boyfriend, you know."

It came out the wrong way and she immediately regretted saying it, but a huge part of her did want to know . . . or maybe just wanted to hear him say what she thought she wanted to hear. Either way, it still made her ashamed. It was horrible gratitude to question someone about their intentions.

Kevin said, "I don't mean to . . . I hope . . ."

"What?" she asked. It came out sounding like a challenge.

"Twice in my life I've been helped by people who had no business helping me. One was a teacher and the other was a stranger. I carry that around with me every day of my life, and I never forget it. I guess I feel I owe the world some payback." He shrugged. "I guess that all sounds pretty dumb."

"That's not dumb."

"I'm really sorry if you thought . . . if I gave you the impression I was, you know . . . after something."

He offered a half-smile and she felt her heart sag. Now there was a reason, plain and simple. Kevin wasn't interested in her; he was just a super-nice guy. And it didn't matter because she had a boyfriend. Matt was her boyfriend.

"I think I'm good now," she said, standing up. She tossed a thumb at the pay phone. "This one isn't working, so I'm sorry to say I'll need to hit the one inside the bar."

"I, uh . . . I'll wait for you at the car."

He turned and started back toward the Camaro. Sarah stood there for a moment, trying to comprehend what had just happened. All night he had been her shadow, and now he was leaving her to fend for herself? She would have thought he would have wanted to protect her inside a bar more than any other place. It wasn't like him at all.

And you know him so well.

She wondered again about his age. Maybe he was under eighteen and knew he couldn't get inside. And if it was something like simple embarrassment, the last thing she wanted to do was push it. She would duck inside, find the phone, and figure out Scotty. After that she would worry about Kevin.

She turned toward the entrance and an involuntary grimace ruined her face. Duncerton was known for basically one thing: Billie's was the only "eighteen" bar in the county. All the underage kids from Centerview migrated there on the weekends, including her friends who were all still under twenty-one. It was the last place she wanted to be, but it was the first recognizable landmark she had spotted after admitting she didn't know where Scotty's brother lived.

"Let the fun begin," she muttered, joining the line of people waiting to get inside. There was some sort of commotion at the door, and she could hear two guys arguing about a misplaced driver's license.

"This guy won't give up," said the girl in front of her. "Hope you're not in a hurry."

It never ends, Sarah thought miserably, resisting the urge to turn and see if Kevin was watching.

[12]

"It's beautiful," Mandy said, sliding the silver bracelet over her wrist. She held out her arm and admired it. "And it's so . . . *me*."

Scott stamped out his cigarette and slouched against the counter. He was relaxed now, the invisible ghosts from earlier not gone, but now in the background. It was sort of like breathing: you only noticed it when you thought about it.

"So you like it?" he asked without much interest.

She bent forward to kiss him and he pulled away in a fake coughing fit. Kissing was okay during sex but not after; then it was sort of like licking an ashtray. It was amazing how much could be ignored or forgotten in the heat of a moment. He also wasn't into that touchy-feely crap. There was no hand holding or snuggling or anything like that. She was okay to be around, but it wasn't like they were going to get married or anything.

"You're too good to me," she said. "Which is how I know you'll go get me a soda."

"Sure." He held out his palm. "Money me."

Her smile dipped. "What happened to the ten I gave you?"

"You never gave me ten."

"Yeah, I did. Last night."

He wiggled his fingers. "You're imagining things. Money, honey."

"I did," she said again, opening the register and fishing out a handful of quarters. Her smile was completely gone as she dumped them into his hand.

"Back in a flash," he said.

She started to say something else about the bracelet, but he didn't bother to listen. It wasn't a big deal. Someone had left it on the table of the restaurant where he had eaten yesterday. That, along with a five-dollar tip. It wasn't his fault the waitresses hadn't bussed the table before he sat down. To the victor went the spoils, as they said. Whatever that meant.

He rounded the corner and shifted his thoughts to the night ahead. The hotel was fairly quiet for a Saturday night, but all that could change at any moment. Fist fights, arguments, men cheating on their wives . . . all the drama anyone could want and more. Last week he had caught two people humping in the hot tub, both of them so drunk they hadn't realized he was standing there watching. There was always something to see, always something to do.

The smell of chlorine filled his nostrils as he entered the pool area. This was the belly of the hotel, his nighttime playground. Pinball machines, Ping-Pong tables, weight room, Jacuzzi . . . everything a growing boy could ever need. He went to the soda machine and fumbled inside his pockets for the quarters.

"Then the pussy started to get in my *face!*"

Scott froze as he saw two guys passing on the other side of the pool. Both had cans of beer and yelped laughter.

"You should have kicked that punk's ass," the other guy said, letting out a loud belch.

Scott stiffened as they looked at him. His hands began to shake and he jammed them in his pockets to make them stop.

"What are you looking at?" the first guy asked, not losing a step. He gave Scott an icy, measured stare, and when they reached the doors on the other side, his buddy said: "You should have kicked *his* ass."

He still heard them when they were out of sight, talking loudly and tossing belches back and forth like a football. When their voices were finally gone, he let out a shaky breath. They had no right talking to him like that. None at all.

He slowly fed the quarters into the machine and hit the button with his fist. When the bottle dropped he punched the button again—this time with more force. Nothing came out, but it felt good.

He started back toward the lobby, and all at once a tremor of fear and anger pushed up inside him. He paused at the hallway door and looked over his shoulder.

"You guys are assholes!" he shouted.

The door wheezed shut behind him as he ran down the hallway as fast as his feet would carry him.

[13]

Kevin sat on the hood of the Camaro with his eyes locked on to the entrance of the bar. He should have gone inside with her but couldn't. Just the thought made him physically ill; another wonderful trait instilled in him by his father.

His hand absently went to his neck, and it took him a moment to realize the cross was gone. It was the first time he had sat in the parking lot of a bar and not had it for reassurance.

It was always the same: the phone call at two in the morning, telling him to come down and pick up his father. Struggling out of bed and into the car, wondering how he was going to get up for school in the morning. If it had been straight back home, it probably would have been okay, but it was always on to some restaurant, where his father would piss and moan between every other bite about how messed up it all was. Nothing in particular—just *all* of it.

He perked up as the doors opened. Two guys staggered out and started toward the rear of the building. Drugs, vomit, or urination was the most likely motivation. There wasn't much he hadn't seen. Once he had witnessed two guys engage in a pissing fight right in front of his car.

"She's coming back out," he reassured himself. "Any second now."

It wasn't like anything was going to happen to her. She was in a public place with loads of people, and when she did come back out, he was going to take her to her friend . . . so why was he sitting there still feeling responsible for her?

You had the perfect opportunity. She flat out asked why you were doing all this, and you blew it.

But what was he supposed to do . . . come right out and say he was attracted to her? And even if he could convince himself that his intentions were honorable, it still felt wrong. She was upset and vulnerable and they both knew it. The last thing he wanted was to make her think he was trying to take advantage of the situation. And then there was the mysterious boyfriend—the boyfriend she hadn't wanted to go back for. Why? Had there been some sort of fight or argument? And if that was the case, why had she mentioned him again? It didn't make sense. The bottom line was that he had to say something, because there was really nothing to lose.

It still settled uneasily inside him, and his lingering bad feeling turned worse when a voice spoke up behind him: "There he is."

It was the guy he had run off earlier, this time flanked by two buddies. Kevin knew he should have expected this—

when you stayed in the same place after a confrontation, it was always construed as a challenge.

"Where's your girl?" the guy shrilled. "Inside the bar? I bet she's never had three guys at once."

The guy flinched as Kevin jumped off the hood. He knew the type well: they got real tough when surrounded by friends. Fortunately, the friends looked no more menacing than the guy. The one on the left was squat and fat, while the other guy had a puff of curly hair that made him look like a giant cotton swab.

"I don't want any trouble," Kevin said, unaware his hands had curled into fists.

"That's too bad," the guy replied, "because you most definitely *got* trouble. Prepare to get stomped."

They came at him.

[14]

Sarah winced at the blast of music that greeted her as the vestibule doors opened and she stepped inside the bar. A hand grabbed her elbow and she jumped.

"License," said the bouncer.

"Sorry," she said, fumbling inside her purse as her gaze swept the bar. Bodies were packed into tight clumps and a thin fog of smoke covered everything.

"Is there a pay phone in here?" she asked.

"By the restrooms near the back." He checked her license. "Show this to the bartender and you'll get a free drink for your birthday."

She thanked him and worked her way into the flow of people. A hand grazed her leg and she whirled to see a knot of college-aged boys grinning at her.

"Coming through!" a voice shouted in her ear as something wet trickled down her shoulder. She sidestepped and bumped into a guy and girl who were making out so fiercely it looked as if they were trying to swallow each other. Sarah stared at them as she moved past, not knowing if it was disgust or jealousy she was feeling. Everyone around her was having a good time, letting off steam and getting crazy. Her mission? Find a phone to call Scotty so she could spend the rest of the night whining about Matt. But was she really that upset anymore? And hadn't she decided that most of it had been her fault?

Yeah, and it's just coincidence that you decide to forgive Matt after you find out Kevin isn't interested in you.

She wondered again if Matt was worried, maybe even waiting at her house with her mother. Which was exactly where she should be. And yet there she was, trying to track down a guy she barely knew anymore, while being chauffeured around by a guy she barely knew at all.

She spotted the phone and turned her attention back to the matter at hand. One thing at a time—*that* was the way things got accomplished. Find Scotty, settle up with Kevin, and move on. That was the plan, plain and simple.

This time there was a directory, and she thumbed it open to the M's. Small towns meant slim books, and she found the listing halfway down the sixth page. *Mason, Wade and Stephanie.*

"Please don't be asleep," she whispered, looking at her watch. She pushed in the coins and tapped out the number. On the sixth ring, a faint and groggy voice answered.

"Wade?" Sarah asked, pressing the phone tightly against her ear. "This is Sarah. Sarah Cate."

There was a small pause and she wondered if he would remember her. They didn't know each extremely well, but she had spent half her childhood with his brother.

"Sarah, sure . . . is everything okay?"

"I'm so sorry to call this late, but I'm trying to find Scotty. Is he there?"

"No, he left earlier."

All the air rushed from her lungs. She was fighting a losing battle.

"He's probably with his girlfriend," Wade said. "She works at the Night Owl on Morningside Drive."

She nodded into the phone. "Thanks. Sorry again for waking you."

"Is everything okay, Sarah?"

"Yeah. Sorry again."

She hung up the phone. That was it, then—one of two things was going to happen. She would either find Scotty at the hotel or dig out her credit card and stay in a room for the night. Regardless, the hotel would be the last stop. The thought made her ill.

Just admit it, her inner voice spoke up. *You can tell yourself whatever you want, but you know that it's Kevin you really want to stay with. Otherwise you would call Matt right now to come pick you up. Or tell Kevin to drive you back home.*

She knew the voice was right: she didn't want to call Matt or find Scotty . . . she didn't want to leave Kevin. It was crazy but true. But did he feel the same?

She studied on this for a moment and a new thought popped into her head: Kevin knew she had a boyfriend, and Kevin was a nice guy. So if Kevin knew she had a boyfriend, and Kevin was a nice guy, would he even attempt to confess his feelings if they existed? Maybe it wasn't all lost; maybe it was up to her to make the first move.

She made her way back toward the entrance, mustering her courage as she went. She would simply ask Kevin if he wanted to see her again after tonight. Or maybe offer to take him to dinner to repay him for everything he had done. Then they could get to know each other better. And from there—

"Sarah?"

It took her a moment to process what she was seeing: Lisa, Jill, and Shannon standing in front of her. It was Jill who had spoken, looking as confused as Sarah felt.

"What are you guys doing here?" Sarah blurted out.

Lisa chuckled. "We're just *out*. Do we need permission?"

"I didn't mean it like that," Sarah began. "I meant—"

"What are you doing here?" Shannon asked. "Shouldn't you be wrapped around Mr. Wonderful back at his apartment?"

"Maybe they already took care of it," Lisa said with a grin. "Check out that nice lump on her forehead. Maybe Matt started porking her brains out and then got bored halfway through and quit."

Shannon and Lisa laughed in chorus; only Jill stayed quiet.

"What is this?" Sarah asked, tears burning her eyes.

"Oh, you hurt her feelings," Shannon said.

"You don't even get it," Lisa hissed. "Do you know how much of an idiot you are? Do you want to know how wonderful your boyfriend is?"

"Don't," Jill chimed in . . . and then shut her mouth as Shannon drilled into her with her eyes.

"I was at Gary's Pizza last Friday," Lisa said, "and Matt came in with a bunch of buddies. He didn't see me, but I heard them talking. One of them asked Matt about that young pretty thing he was with, and Matt laughed and asked which one. He said he had two of them going at the same time." Lisa's face wrinkled as she imitated his voice. "*But if you're talking about Sarah, mark my words: I'll get what I want on her birthday, one way or another.*"

Shannon said, "What comes around goes around."

"I hope it was really special," Lisa said in disgust. "Just don't expect to come crawling back to us after he dumps your dumb ass."

The tears came fast and hard as Sarah blindly pushed her way through the crowd and escaped into the bathroom.

[15]

"I don't get it," said Scott.

"She'd shop for people."

"Who would pay your mother to do their shopping?" he asked.

"Lots of people," Mandy said. "She got the idea from a talk show. Some people can't leave their house because of an illness or disability, so she'd go to the grocery store for them or run other errands. That's the business she's going to start, and I'm going to help her."

"What is this world coming to?" Scott said, picking up her lighter. "But now that you say that, I swear I read once about a service where someone will sit by your hospital bed while you're dying of cancer, or something along those lines. Some people don't have families, and no one wants to die alone. Maybe your mom could pick up some extra bucks doing that."

"Nasty," Mandy said with a grunt.

"How could you sit next to someone while they're wasting away? I suppose it's a good thing, though. Not the dying part, but someone wanting to help."

Mandy shrugged and began flipping through a stack of papers.

"I had a buddy whose uncle was dying of cancer," Scott said. "His uncle eventually had to go to the hospital, and when my buddy went up to visit, he saw the drop-dead gorgeous nurse that was caring for him. My buddy started going there every day, just to see the nurse, and his uncle never knew the truth—that his nephew was there for her, not him. And when his uncle died, he died happy, because he felt loved. Nothing came of anything with my buddy and the nurse, but his uncle . . ."

Scott looked into his hands, tracing the scars and lines with his eyes.

"Wasn't that a good thing?" he asked. "I mean, even if it was for the wrong reasons, it still counts for something . . . doesn't it?"

They both looked up as the lobby doors swung open. The man in the doorway was tall, slender, and cloaked in a trench coat as dark as the night. A small goatee framed the lower half of his face, and the part in his hair was as exact as a freshly raked garden. His eyes stayed on Scott as he approached the counter.

"I require a room."

"One sec," Mandy said, disappearing into the back office. The man turned his gaze back to Scott, who gave a friendly nod.

"Should I know you?" the man asked.

Scott dropped his eyes and skulked to one of the chairs in the corner.

Mandy returned with a handful of registration slips and set one on the counter. "Fill out your name, address, license plate—"

"No car."

A mechanical smile perched her lips. "Then I guess you wouldn't fill that part out now, would you?"

Scott grinned under his hand. Mandy was an expert bitch, especially at work. It was the badge of a person who had gone through the motions too many times to count, an *I've done customer service my whole life* trait. It wasn't learned, but earned.

"Do you take this attitude with all your prospective clientele?" the man asked, not looking up as he scribbled. "Does it make you feel superior in some way?"

Scott felt the grin slide from his face.

"Do you not believe that as a customer in your establishment, a certain level of respect should be given? Or is that too much to expect of someone who works at the minimum wage level and has chosen a career that barely requires a grammar school education?"

"What does that mean?" Mandy snapped.

"Tell me, little girl, why would you want to risk agitating someone you don't know? You have no idea who I am, let alone what I am capable of. I am a mere stranger at this moment, captured only by your eyes and the surveillance camera on the wall. I am fairly certain the camera is a mere ornament to deter thievery, and I'm absolutely certain that you do not possess the intellect to remember my face. So I ask you to think carefully about how you have behaved just now, because in a moment I'm going to reach into my pocket, and if you're lucky, I will be pulling out only my wallet . . . and not a knife to cut your throat ear to ear."

The man pushed the registration card back at her with one finger. Mandy diverted her gaze toward Scott and opened her mouth.

"And who have we here?" the man asked, turning his head. "Your boyfriend, I presume? Are you expecting him to step up and say something?"

Scott slunk down in his seat.

"You have something to interject?" the man asked.

"No," Scott croaked.

The man smiled at Mandy. "Then our business here is near completion. I require a single room, smoking, preferably near a side entrance. Are you retaining this, or shall I write it down so it can be deciphered at your leisure?"

"No," Mandy said quietly, tapping away at the keyboard. "Ninety-eight dollars and twenty-seven cents."

The man produced an immaculate hundred-dollar bill and set it on the counter. Mandy waited until his hand was back at his side before taking the bill and gathering his change.

"Room 130," she said, setting the key card in front of him.

"A pleasure," the man said with a wooden smile. The key card disappeared into his pocket and he left with barely a sound. Scott heaved himself up from the chair and sneaked a look around the corner.

"Thanks for sticking up for me," Mandy hissed. "What if he *had* pulled out a knife? Would you have just run off and let him kill me?"

"He was only shitting you. You're just pissed because he made you look like an idiot."

"Screw you," she spat. The phone rang and she grabbed it: "Front desk."

Scott reached for the registration card and knocked over the Styrofoam cup of coffee next to the ashtray.

"Yes, right away," Mandy said with a scowl, slamming down the phone. "Scott—"

"Albert Spyder," he said, showing her. "That doesn't sound like a real name, does it?"

"I forgot to check his license," she said irritably, grabbing a roll of paper towels from under the counter. "Asshole."

Her breasts jiggled side to side as she wiped up the coffee, and Scott realized he was getting aroused again. She caught his stare and her face clouded.

"No way. Room 111 needs towels and then I have to make my rounds before doing an assload of paperwork."

"Doing an assload," he said with a grin. "I like the sound of that."

She glared at him as she came out from behind the counter. "Just stay out of trouble until I get back. Think you can handle that for five minutes?"

He counted off his fingers. "Five . . . got it."

"I didn't know you could count that high," she said over her shoulder. "I'm impressed."

He jabbed his middle finger after her as she went. Out of the corner of his eye he saw the surveillance camera and gave that the finger as well. Stupid thing wasn't real anyway.

He collapsed back into the chair and glanced at the newspaper on the table beside him. LOCAL MAN FOUND DEAD was printed in giant letters across the first page. He quickly scanned the article: body found in alley behind Chestnut Street . . . white male seen lingering in the area earlier . . . police had no suspects . . .

"Great," he said. Chestnut Street was only two blocks from the hotel.

He turned away and tried to clear his mind. Being murdered was the last thing he needed to worry about; there were a whole host of other problems directly within himself.

The worst were his eyes: burning and itching from what felt like hot splinters jabbing from the inside. All he needed was a quick nap and he'd be good as new.

He wiggled in his seat, trying to get comfortable. Every bump in the vinyl seemed to poke a different part of his body, and even the armrests felt hard and impersonal. He exhaled and closed his eyes. The darkness was swift and cruel and his heart began to speed up. He could sense someone coming and forced himself not to open his eyes. It was all in his head. Nothing was wrong.

His breath informed him otherwise, clogging his throat and popping open his mouth.

"Come on," he muttered. "Keep it together."

If things got any worse, he was going to end up talking to someone who jotted in a notepad and charged by the hour. When you couldn't close your eyes for a few seconds, it was time to do something.

"Just a phase," he told himself.

He didn't remind himself that the phase had been going on for months, and the only time he truly slept was when his body shut down on him from exhaustion. Last week Mandy had found him asleep on the toilet with his pants around his ankles. He had made up some story about not sleeping the night before because of a party or something, and she never brought it up again. She knew he had trouble sleeping, but not to the degree it ran. It wasn't like he was about to tell her everything that went on in his life. Once you started sharing stuff like that, people looked at you funny and didn't return your calls.

The phone on the counter rang and he straightened. Once . . . twice . . . he counted them off until the answering machine kicked in. Mandy was taking forever.

He settled back into the chair, exhaustion working its way up his legs and stealing into his arms. He told himself he wasn't going to try to sleep . . . he was only going to sit there and relax and try to shut down his brain a little. Sometimes that was almost the same as a nap. No one was going to come into the lobby; nothing was going to happen. And once Mandy came back, he would piss away the time with her and not think about bodies in alleys, or men with knives in their pockets, or Chestnut Street—

He concentrated on thinking about nothing and let his mind drift. Relaxing your eyelids was just a really long blink . . . it didn't mean you were trying to sleep.

He closed his eyes.

It wasn't like he was letting down his defense or anything . . . he was still as awake as ever . . . he was just blinking . . . a really . . . long . . .

The smell of smoke tickled his nose, and he let out a hearty sneeze.

"Bless you."

Scott bolted upright; the man from earlier was sitting in the chair beside him, holding a lit cigar.

"Do you know why people speak that?" asked the man. "That is to say: do you know why the blessing is said?"

"Your heart stops," Scott stammered, barely aware of the words leaving his mouth. "They're thanking God when it starts again."

The man grinned. "When your heart stops, it gives the Devil a chance to sneak in. *That* is why the blessing is said: to ward off evil."

A curl of smoke crawled from the man's open mouth; the teeth inside looked like tiny chipped headstones.

"She's running some towels to a room," Scott said quickly.

"And I am waiting for a cab," said the man. "Does this help somehow, now that we have exchanged this information?"

Scott slid further down into the chair and fumbled out his cigarettes.

"Ah, yes," said the man with another grin, "what marvelous creatures of habit we are to indulge in a practice that leaves behind only decay and disease. Tell me, does it not strike you as odd that people feel the need to manufacture death when it is so accessible?"

"Uh, I guess—"

"And what else have we discovered?" asked the man. He lifted the edge of the newspaper and raised an eyebrow. "Local man found dead on Chestnut Street . . . is that far from here, I wonder?"

"Two blocks," Scott whispered.

"It says the coroner purported the death a heart attack." The man laughed. "At first the headline led me to believe it was a murder of sorts . . . but wait a moment . . . now this is interesting. A witness said the man's eyes had filled with blood—a most peculiar side effect for a victim of heart attack. Very interesting, indeed. What could do that to a man, I wonder? Perhaps he saw something . . . ghastly?"

Scott swallowed and said nothing.

"I saw something ghastly once," whispered the man. "Would you care to hear the tale?"

"I should go," Scott said, rising from the chair.

"Do I make you uncomfortable? I assure you that is not my intention."

"No. It's . . . I just get tired of sitting sometimes."

"Then by all means, please stand. It is a refreshing change. Most of my day is spent with people who sit. I'm a doctor of the mind, you see. A head *shrinker*, if you will. People pay to tell me their fears. Can you imagine?"

"Yeah," Scott said, forcing out a laugh. "Crazy."

"It was a year ago on this very eve," said the man. "I was in my office, working late, and a young man—no more than a boy, really—found his way into my chambers. He was most distraught and reluctant to speak, and it was only after several moments of rambling that his tale began to unfold. He believed in his heart that he had wronged another—"

"Wronged?"

The man looked amused. "Done wrong to. Caused harm. Caused . . . *death*."

"Oh."

"How this occurred, the boy would not say. Truth be told, it was of little consequence to me, for I was much more troubled by what was spoken next. You see, because of this occurrence, the boy believed he was being . . . *haunted*. He believed that God had returned the dead to punish him for his sin."

The man paused to draw from the cigar. Scott realized he was still standing and sat back down.

"The boy grew more agitated with each passing minute," said the man, "and I found myself at a loss. There was no question he was quite disturbed, yet I was ill-equipped to handle an illness of this severity. I excused myself and escaped to an adjoining room to call a colleague. However, before I so much as touched the phone receiver, the lights winked out and the room was seized by blackness.

"Silence washed over the air. As the seconds passed and my eyes struggled to recapture their focus, it was as if the room itself had come alive.

"The wind moaned through the open windows, moving a jacket on the wall. Long shadows danced silently across the floor. I became aware of a smell, an odor so foul it seemed to burn the very edge of my tongue with each inhale. The imagination can be a quite powerful tool—this I know better than most—and yet before I could resign myself to believe it was all in my mind, the jacket on the wall moved again . . . only I realized it wasn't a jacket at all.

"Someone was standing in the corner.

"The figure stood motionless, the shadows of the night camouflaging its face. No sound escaped its mouth, not even a whisper of breath. I told myself to call out—surely this was only another lost soul in search of aid—but I could not speak. It was as if the cords in my throat had been severed by an invisible blade.

"Finally I could take no more, and just as I began to summon my words, the being moved forward with a sudden urgency, as if some silent command had been called forth.

"Then it was gone through the doorway.

"If there were words to describe the terror I had just embraced, they were out of my grasp. And before my mind could fully rationalize what had transpired, there was a sharp crack of sound from my chambers: a gunshot.

"I leaped forward, my heart thundering within my chest. Unseen hands pushed me down the hallway until I was standing at the entrance.

"The boy was a corpse on the floor. Next to his hand lay a revolver, just out of reach, and for a bare moment, I saw what appeared to be a figure standing over his body . . . and then it simply vanished."

Scott stiffened as the man stabbed out his cigar in the ashtray. Puffs of smoke and ash filled the air.

"The authorities were summoned, and within the hour the office was a swarm of activity. There was little speculation that anything other than suicide was the cause of death, but the arrival of the coroner soon proved something unexpected: there was no blood discovered on his person. That is to say, there was no gunshot wound."

Scott blinked. "Huh?"

"There was no blood, you see, because the boy hadn't shot into himself. The revolver had been fired at the doorway."

The man tapped his ashes.

"The coroner purported the death a heart attack. 'How bizarre an irony,' his assistant said, 'to have your heart seize a mere instant before taking your own life.' As for myself, I didn't know what to believe. It simply looked as if the boy had been . . . *frightened* to death."

A car horn barked outside. Scott watched helplessly as the man stood.

"To this very day," said the man, "I can still see that figure. And I find myself praying it truly was only a trick of my mind: a figment of my imagination. Because I would hate to believe that I saw something else . . . something that came back from the dead to take care of unfinished business."

The man grinned.

"You take care now. That is to say, care for those things that go bump in the night. But surely you have nothing to fear, not someone as young and *innocent* as yourself."

The doors flew open and the man disappeared . . . and when the phone rang again, Scott nearly screamed.

[16]

The knock on the bathroom stall door was followed by a timid voice: "Sarah, will you please come out?"

"Go away, Jill."

"I want to talk." The door handle jiggled. "I know Lisa was upset, but she shouldn't have said that stuff."

"Then it was a lie?"

There was only silence from the other side. Sarah snapped off the lock and let the door swing open.

"No," Jill said quietly. "I heard it too. It was near the end of my shift, and Lisa was out visiting me."

"You work at the pizza place?"

"For over a month now. Sarah, do you know how long it's been since we've talked? Do you know how many times I've been by your house to see you, or tried calling you?"

Sarah's eyes drifted to the floor.

"Do you know you blew off Shannon's party last month? Remember, the four of us were supposed to go out to the cabin? Shannon paid for everything, and all you had to do was show up. What was so important that night? She left you a bunch of messages. You had to have known about it."

"Matt," Sarah whispered. "He had a really bad day and didn't want to be alone."

"Try asking Lisa about feeling alone. You crushed her when you stopped going to the bookstore to visit her on her breaks. Do you know how much she looked forward to that? No matter how crappy of a night she was having, she could always count on you to make her laugh."

"So the joke's on me," Sarah said, moving past Jill to the sink. "I've been blowing you all off for Matt, so now you all have your revenge."

"That's not it at all."

"Then what am I supposed to think?"

"You didn't let me finish what I was saying," Jill said, raising her voice. For the first time there was a hint of anger there. "I didn't know what to do at first. Lisa said it was poetic justice and it served you right, but it made me sick to my stomach just thinking about it. I left a message the next day and said it was important that I talk to you, but you never called me back."

Jill shivered and ran her hands down her arms.

"We've all been friends for so long," she continued. "I kept telling myself you weren't meaning to blow us off . . . that you were just wrapped up in the moment of someone new and exciting. I don't hate you for it. I could never hate you, Sarah. You've just been blinded these last few months, that's all. Blinded by someone you thought was special."

Sarah opened her mouth and then closed it.

"And maybe it was just talk," Jill said with a half-shrug. "You know how guys are when they're out together. They have to talk trash, don't they?"

"Sure," Sarah said briefly.

A small silence settled between them.

"What will you do?" Jill asked.

"About what?"

"About everything, I guess."

After a pause, Sarah answered, "I don't know."

"Will you call Lisa and Shannon?"

Sarah ran her hands under the faucet and pressed them against her cheeks. The cool water immediately sprang some life back into her.

"I know it was wrong to blow them off," Sarah said, "and part of me knew I was doing it . . ."

"But?"

"But I didn't intentionally try to hurt them. What they said and did out there . . . nobody deserved that."

"People strike out in different ways when they're hurt. Maybe they just don't know any better."

Sarah looked at herself in the mirror as she thought of her mother.

"Matt *didn't* do that to your head, did he?"

"Kevin," Sarah whispered. He was waiting for her in the parking lot. She had completely forgotten.

"Who's Kevin?"

Sarah started for the door. "I have to go."

"Wait." Jill pulled a yellow envelope from her purse and shoved it into Sarah's hand. "Happy birthday, Sarah."

She left without another word. Inside the envelope was a birthday card, along with a gift certificate for Sarah's favorite pizza place.

"Remember," Sarah read, "you can't make everyone happy. You're not pizza."

Sarah tucked the card into her pocket, trying to smile but not quite able to.

[17]

Scott braced his hands against the sides of the toilet and closed his eyes against the colorful mess of vomit floating inside. He had barely made it into the bathroom. He hit the flusher with a shaky hand; everything inside was sucked away by the water tornado.

I do blame you, a voice whispered.

He tried to shut the voice off—it was all bullshit. The man and his story, the voices inside his head . . . he wasn't going to let it take over. He had suffered enough.

"All shit," Scott panted, his mind already forming the images in his head. He rubbed his eyes as if to push it away, but it was too late: it played like a movie in his mind . . .

Driving through the local burger joint, his dad behind the wheel. Cut off by some fancy hotrod while pulling out of the drive-through onto the street. Scott's food spilling from his lap onto the floor. Scott screaming obscenities out the window and throwing his drink at the hotrod in a fit of rage. His dad warning Scott that his anger was going to catch up with him someday and offering his own food. Scott refusing and lighting a cigarette, wishing everyone in the world would simply disappear. Their car suddenly squealing to a stop and his dad grabbing at his chest; both knew what a heart attack looked like—it had happened twice before. Scott climbing out of the car, running over to the driver side. Another car screeching to a stop behind them: the college kids in the hotrod. No time to explain about his dad before the fists beat down on him, driving him to the ground in a flurry of punches.

Blackness . . .

Waking up surrounded by police, watching his dad taken away in the back of the ambulance without its lights flashing or sirens blaring.

"It was an accident," Scott moaned. "It wasn't my fault."

He lay on the floor, wishing he was dead.

[18]

It all seemed too easy now, and Sarah tried her hardest not to over-analyze. Matt was a fading blur in her head, Kevin was waiting for her at the car, and Jill had forgiven her. All her guilt was buried. All her insecurities were on pause. Her stomach felt calm. Nothing was going to ruin it for her; everything was in perfect focus.

Kevin *liked* her—she acknowledged this now. The Matt thing had clouded it a little, but in the end, it hadn't been able to black it out. In one swoop she had patted it on the butt and sent it on its way. She had just needed some extra information to convince herself beyond a reasonable doubt that she and Matt weren't meant to be. Matt would have been proud of her, analyzing the data and all that crap. Asshole.

Her world fell flat again when she stepped outside and saw Kevin's car surrounded by people. She quickened her step, taking in the murmur of the crowd.

". . . got the crap kicked out of them . . ."

". . . quickest fight I ever saw . . ."

"... blood ..."

"Let me by," Sarah pleaded, pushing her way through. Her heart was hammering in her chest, drowning out all sounds. "Please. Let me through."

She reached the Camaro. Kevin was sitting on the bumper with his elbows on his knees. His breathing was labored and fast.

"What happened?" she asked.

"Nothing. Can we go now?"

"You should have seen it," a girl with pink hair told Sarah. "Your boyfriend is off the hook. He just destroyed three dudes in a matter of *seconds*."

Sarah bit back tears when she saw the red sandpaper marks on Kevin's knuckles. "It was that guy, wasn't it? He came back while I was inside."

"It doesn't matter. It's done."

Kevin teetered forward as he stood, and Sarah slipped a hand around his waist, pulling up the corner of his shirt and exposing a golf-ball-sized bruise.

"Oh my God, Kevin, you're hurt."

"I'm not hurt."

"But your stomach—"

"They didn't do that. It was already there." He lowered his eyes and his voice went tight. "Can we just get out of here now?"

He pulled away and made his way to the driver side, using the car for support. Sarah climbed inside and flinched when he slammed his door.

"Did you use the phone?" Kevin asked. His fingers were locked around the steering wheel and his knuckles had changed from red to white.

"Yes," she answered quietly. "Night Owl Hotel."

"And do you know where *that's* at?"

She nodded. "Yes."

Kevin jammed the Camaro into reverse, barely glancing into the rearview mirror as he tore backward out of the stall. They shot onto the street, and it took all of Sarah's resolve to hold back her tears.

[19]

Scott washed his hands a third time, trying to scrub away the stickiness from his palms. Guys had no aim, especially in public bathrooms. The worst was underneath the wall urinals: you could always count on seeing a small yellow puddle between your feet. The trick was not to stand in it when you peed, because it turned the bottom of your shoes into suction cups when you walked away. The only successful technique was to straddle your legs as you did your business, which was so awkward it usually helped contribute to the small lake on the floor. It was a vicious cycle.

Scott thought about all this as he washed, purposely trying to clutter his mind and not focus on his body. Something wasn't right. Most times he felt like he was on overload, as if there were too many circuits operating at once. He always imagined himself as a Christmas tree with bulbs that kept burning brighter until they were on the verge of exploding like firecrackers. Now he felt as if his whole body might just shut down. His lungs would fail; his heart would stop beating; his brain would stop working . . . something.

He imagined himself as a plastic kiddy pool that had a small leak.

"Just need sleep," he reassured himself, but his hand was unsteady as it snatched paper towels from the dispenser. He stared at himself in the mirror as he dried. His eyes were on the brink of sinking into the back of his head, and the thin face his mother had cursed him with was too hollow, his cheeks the aftermath of two tiny cave-ins. His skin was so pale it was almost illuminated in the glass.

"You're dying," he said.

He squinted at his reflection, challenging the mirror image to react. There was nothing. No dropping of the jaw, no gasp of surprise, no dramatic hand gestures of any sort . . . only a trickle of sweat dribbling down into his left eyebrow. In high school he always told people he wasn't going to live past the age of twenty-one. There was no basis or reason for it—it was just something he said. A stupid thing to make him sound cool . . . to spit in the eye of death and say *Screw you and bring it on*. But now it didn't seem cool at all. Twenty-one was only a few months away. Why had he picked that age? Had it been some sort of premonition?

"Bullshit," he croaked.

There were no ghosts and no supernatural haunts. Discharging his stomach had put things back into perspective and given him time to catalog. Something was wrong with him, but he didn't know what; his dad was dead and it wasn't his fault; he had fallen asleep and imagined the man with the cigar. There was no other way to explain it. It seemed ridiculous to him now to think that some *man* would suddenly appear and rattle off a tale of ghosts and goblins. How convenient and coincidental was that? He had dozed off without realizing it, and all the shit in his head had teamed up and acted out a small play before exiting stage left. How could he have been so stupid to think otherwise? He couldn't even remember leaving the lobby and coming into the bathroom; he had still probably been half-asleep.

He knocked a cigarette into his hand and stared at it curiously as a new thought popped into his head: maybe smoking was the cause of all his problems. Any idiot knew it wasn't good for the body, and he had been pursuing the habit for years. *Another nail for the coffin*, as his mother would say. He had heard it so many times it was etched into his brain, and he couldn't begin to count how often she had hidden clippings about the hazards of smoking inside his cigarette packs or slipped magazine articles under his bedroom door. She had been relentless, even going so far as placing nicotine gum and patches into his pockets after doing his laundry. Eventually she had resigned the crusade and resorted to stuffing cigarette *coupons* into his pockets, because if he wasn't going to quit, he might as well be saving money. Somehow, that made it worse. It was as if she had simply given up on him. She was good at giving up. He still remembered how she had given up on their dad. The divorce had been sudden and unexpected, shortly after his eighteenth birthday. "Sometimes people fall out of love," was all that his dad would say. It was a shit explanation and he hated them both for it. He never forgave her for leaving them, and the few times she did call, he refused to speak to her. She kept at it for a while and then simply stopped trying to reach him. It was the smoking thing all over again: she simply gave up.

"I hope you're happy," he huffed, anger splashing over him. "You should have tried harder. You never give up on people. I'm messed up in the head and my body is dying, and I . . . blame . . . *you*."

He watched himself closely, daring his other self to speak. The moments ticked away with neither of them moving.

"Screw you," he whispered.

He kicked the garbage can and it clattered across the bathroom floor, leaving behind a trail of used paper towels.

Your head is a scary place. It's sort of like a never-ending game of connect the dots that don't really connect.

He finished off the cigarette in silence, listening to the steady knock of his heartbeat. As long as his heart was pounding, he was okay. He didn't know if heart attacks were hereditary or earned, but he would be keeping tabs on it. Nothing else mattered as long as his blood kept thumping.

"And no ghosts," he told himself, taking a moment to run his hands through his hair. There was some color back in his cheeks and he actually felt a little better. Physical problems could at least be dealt with. He might even pick up a phone and schedule a check-up with a doctor. It couldn't hurt, and then he would know for sure. He went to the door and yanked it open, momentarily feeling better.

"Scott," Mandy said, grabbing his arm the second he stepped into the lobby. "We got a problem."

He gave her a blank stare. The last thing in the world he was concerned with was her problems.

"I forgot my pills at home," she said, as if it was his fault. "I take my pill at midnight."

"And?"

She balked. "Don't you remember screwing me?"

"Barely," he said with a shrug.

"Let me spell it out for you," she said in a low, controlled voice. "I need my pills, unless you want to be a daddy."

"Take it tomorrow," he told her. "It's okay as long as you take it within twenty-four hours, right?"

But all at once it sank in. There was a chance she was going to be pregnant if he didn't fix the situation. She could be pregnant, and either he would have to get enough money for an abortion or she would have a baby. Then she would want to be married.

"How could you forget?" he asked with a whimper.

"How could I *forget*?" she mimicked, raising her voice. "Did you seriously just ask me that? I can't take much more of this, Scott. I swear to *God*, I'm going to leave you if you can't get your shit together."

He gaped at her, barely hearing her words, as Mandy's features twisted and changed . . . until he was staring into the face of his mother.

"You heard me," the Mandy-mother said. "*Leave* you. No one wants you, Scott. You're shit. You're no good. How could anyone love you? Why would anyone *want* you?"

One hand jumped to his stomach and the other to his mouth; he could feel his insides crawling up into his throat. He was going to lose everything again.

"Scott?" she asked, reaching out.

He broke into a coughing fit as spit flew from his mouth. Mandy took a step toward him, and he shook his head violently as his stomach roiled again.

"Water," he rasped, refusing to look at her.

She grabbed for the water bottle on the counter, and he lowered himself to the floor as his breaths came in thin clumps.

"Here," she said.

He drank half of it in one gulp and closed his eyes against a push of dizziness. It was a distant feeling, as he faintly became aware of a floating sensation. He snapped his head forward and sucked in great gasps of air, trying to grab himself back.

"Scott?"

He leaned forward and wiped his mouth on the sleeve of his jacket. It left a dark greenish mark: a combination of spit and snot.

"Are you okay?" she asked.

He slowly lifted his head and saw what he expected: Mandy, and only Mandy.

It's because you were just thinking about your mother in the bathroom. In your present state we can't be trusted—

"You need those pills," he said, working his way to his feet. He used her arm to balance himself. "It really rattled me to think you could be . . ."

She stared at him with uncertainty.

"Give me your apartment key and I'll get the pills," he told her.

She hesitated for a moment and then reached over the counter for her purse.

You're a textbook case waiting to be written, his new companion warned.

"Here," she said, thrusting the key at him.

"Where are the pills?"

"Inside the bathroom medicine cabinet. Do you even remember how to get to my place?"

He started toward the door. "I'll figure it out."

"Scott . . . is something wrong inside you?"

He stopped. His head turned, but he didn't look at her. "What do you mean?"

"Do you have a condition or something? Like a medical thing?"

An odd sensation came over him: it was as if he had stepped outside of his body. His other self could see Mandy watching him, a motherly, concerned look etched into her face.

She said, "Because one minute you're normal—even sweet at times—and then the next minute . . ."

She frowned.

"Maybe something inside you is broken," she finished. "Have you ever thought of that?"

"No," he said quietly. "I've never thought about it."

He left her standing there without looking back.

[20]

Sarah shook her head again at the stalled train that blocked the road; she could literally see the Night Owl Hotel through the gaps of the train cars. Things kept going from bad to worse . . . or maybe the cosmos were giving her one last chance to make things right. She had tried to inject some small talk between her and Kevin during the drive, but a series of grunts and nods was all she had been able to cajole.

She took out her last cigarette and looked at it. It was crimped in several places but still smoke-able. It had been through a lot with her that night, and she was happy to put it out of its misery. She only wished she could do the same for herself.

"Why do you smoke?"

She turned, startled by the sound of his voice. There was no expression on his face, and she wondered how someone so giving could also be so guarded.

"I don't really," she answered. "Part-time gig. And I made a promise to quit on my birthday."

"When is that?"

She checked her watch. "It ended seventeen minutes ago."

He nodded. Then he was gone again, staring out the driver side window. It was a start, but a far cry from before.

He turned out to be a jerk just like all the rest of them, the voice inside her sniped. *You're not even dating him, and he's already pushing you around emotionally.*

She promptly told the voice to shut the hell up—she had too many other thoughts running laps inside her head to play games with her mind. First and foremost was the bruise on his stomach. She desperately wanted to talk about it, and it was taking all of her willpower not to ask. How did you make someone talk when they didn't want to?

And then it came to her.

"Do you think you'll write about this?" she asked.

He looked at her, and for a brief instant she felt a glimmer of hope. The idea came straight from her psychology class during her one semester of college: one way to align two enemies was to find a greater *common* enemy . . . or a common interest. They were far from enemies, but they were divided. Writing was his passion, and it was her way back in. Her teacher would have been proud. Even if it did feel like a dirty trick.

Her satisfaction was short-lived, however; he didn't seem to be biting. His eyes were locked on her, and again she found herself unable to read anything on his face.

"I was just wondering," she asked timidly. "I do want to read some of your writing, and I thought it'd be cool to read about something that really happened. And if you write the same way you talk—"

"How do I talk?" he asked.

A small smile threatened to jump to her lips and she forced it back down. She finally had his attention; now all she had to do was sustain it.

"Like a writer," she finished casually. "You have a way with words. I always have stories in my head, and I'd love to try writing them down, but I don't know how. It's like I don't know how to write."

He cocked an eyebrow at her. "Anyone can write," he said . . . and she knew she had him. His face had softened and there wasn't exactly a smile on his lips, but it wasn't a frown. At that moment they were on level ground, and she wasn't about to lose momentum.

"It's not just that," she said, shaking her head. "I don't know all the grammar stuff and rules. I wouldn't know where to end a chapter or where to start a new paragraph. Most people take classes to learn that stuff, right?"

He was shaking his head. "I learned to write by reading. Eventually you get a feel for the language and how things work. Writing really is nothing more than putting words down on paper. And don't worry if it's garbage. First drafts always are. What most people don't understand is ninety percent of writing is rewriting. You have to keep working at the story—molding it like a piece of clay.”

“But how do you make it into something?”

“How do you mean?”

“How do you tell a story? Most of my writing is either just my feelings or some random scene that would be in the middle of a story. I wouldn’t know how to begin to structure a story.”

“Well, you obviously have a beginning and an ending,” he said, holding both index fingers in the air. He paused, looked at the dashboard, and pulled some coins from the ashtray. She hid another smile under her hand. The tone of the whole conversation was almost business-like, but not in a bad way.

“Look at these coins,” he said, motioning to the five coins he had placed on the dashboard. He pointed to the ones on each end. “This is your beginning and your end.”

“Okay . . .”

“And these are things that have to happen,” he said, touching each of the three coins in the middle. “*Important* events that shape the story and help move it toward the climax.”

“What kind of things?” she asked.

“Conflicts, problems; things like that.”

“Like a guy finding a girl stranded by the side of a road?”

For a moment she thought she had outsmarted herself—all at once he became a statue. She watched him carefully as he cleared his throat and swallowed.

"Sure," he said heavily. "That would be considered the *first* important thing that happens."

"And the second coin is them searching all night for her friend?"

Again, he hesitated, and she realized she was holding in a breath.

"If so," he slowly continued, "that brings us to the last coin, which is him dropping her off at a hotel. So the only question that remains is 'what happens at the end?'"

"What does happen?"

"You always have an idea about the ending, but it doesn't always turn out that way. The most important thing isn't working through the main events to reach the conclusion . . . it's the little stuff in between. Little things that maybe aren't essential to the plot of the story, but essential to other things, like getting to know the people and their motivations."

"Why is that most important?"

"Because regardless of what happens to the people, the story will still always progress and reach a conclusion. Time will always pass. Just like real life. It's *how* that time is spent, and the things that are said and done that are important. What people do or don't do . . ."

His brow hardened as he trailed off, and she realized she was losing him.

"So now I know the tricks," she said, "but that still doesn't mean I can write well. How do you get good?"

"Practice," he said, turning back toward the window.

She shot a nervous glance at the train. It was only a matter of time before it started to move, and then she'd be out of luck.

"But you need talent, don't you? I mean, they say everybody is good at something. I love to read. And I would love to write stories, but what if I try and they're no good? At least by not doing it, I'll never know. Isn't it better that way?"

"You don't mean that."

"Why not?" she asked with a humorless laugh. "It's not like anything else has worked out for me. I clearly have no luck with guys, college wasn't for me, and I can't land a decent job. I'm just a screw-up."

It was supposed to be a half-joke for stealing sympathy, but what wasn't true about it? She was twenty-one, still living at home, and worked part-time in a movie theater. Her longest relationship had been a whopping three months; one change of a season.

"I know all about screw-ups," he said softly. "Sarah, you're not even close. I hope you don't think that."

"It's just so hard."

"Hard?"

This is it, she told herself.

She opened her mouth and felt a catch in her throat; the train was starting to move. She fumbled for words, her concentration now completely broken. The clanging of the gate arms grew louder, beating into her head.

"Not hard," she said. "*Difficult.*"

He raised his eyebrows.

"You're so confident," she continued. "You already know what you want to do with your life and you're so young . . . just a kid, really. I just wish I had it all together like you."

She attacked a strand of hair with her fingers, trying to find the words. The train began to pick up speed. She sneaked a glance at him, saw the frown on his face, and knew something was wrong. She backtracked through what she had said . . . and realized she had called him a kid.

Panic swept through her as she saw the hurt in his eyes. She knew he had to be younger than she was, but she didn't care about that. The whole thing was supposed to come out as a compliment.

"Hey," she said, touching his shoulder. "I didn't mean anything by that."

"You don't have to explain anything to me. This whole night has been about me wanting to pay it forward and help you out. That's all. You don't need to apologize for anything."

Her heart sank at his words, and she could tell by his face that he didn't mean it. "Kevin, I—"

"The train's moving now," he said with a pained smile. "You'll be where you want to be soon."

"It's not like that."

"Sure. I don't mean to be rude, Sarah, but those train gates are giving me a headache, and I don't really feel like talking right now. Sorry."

Kevin, you're breaking my heart, she thought to herself.

She slid down in her seat, determined to never open her mouth again.

[21]

"Hell, no," Scott said under his breath.

He jammed the key back into the lock and cranked on it with more force. If Mandy had given him the wrong key, he couldn't be held responsible for what he did when he got back to the hotel. Things were getting *way* too high maintenance, and after this "pregnancy" charade was played out, he would be taking a hard, serious look at his options. No one ever said anything about having a baby.

"Come on," he hissed. The key threatened to bend under the pressure as he bore down harder. "Turn, you son-of-a—"

The lock spun and the door swung open. He jerked back a step, half-expecting something or someone to come rushing out, but there was only the shadow of the door.

"I'm not a murderer," he said loudly. Mandy kept a roommate and the last thing he needed was to get clocked by a baseball bat. "Mandy gave me her key. I'm just here to get something for her."

He lingered in the hallway, wanting nothing more than to turn around and forget the whole thing. All their time was spent at the hotel, and that was exactly the way he wanted it. But this was different. This was Mandy's life: the place she slept and ate. When you started going to a girl's apartment it made things more personal, and he had no interest in that. It wasn't like he was going to hang out there with her or spend the night or anything. Sleep was impossible enough without having another body crammed into the bed.

"Hello?" he said, poking his head into the apartment. "Anyone home?"

The place appeared empty. He stepped inside and locked the door behind him. You couldn't be too safe in this day and age.

Medicine cabinet, he reminded himself.

He moved down the hallway. Dirty dishes balanced on every flat surface in sight, and garments of clothing were strewn everywhere, as if a hamper bomb had gone off in the middle of the living room. Even the kitchen counter had been breached by shirts and socks.

The bathroom reeked of pungent perfumes and soaps, and he did his best to ignore the smell as he opened the medicine cabinet and stared at the mess inside. There were remedies for everything: pills to make you sleep, tablets to fight nausea, creams to cover pimples . . . it went on and on. And in the top left corner: one green plastic birth-control dispenser.

"All this fuss for you," he said.

Until that night, he had never known it was the pill she was on. He knew *some* sort of birth control was involved (after their first romp, she told him they were "safe" and had nothing to worry about), but she had never offered any specifics. Now he was part of the process and that wasn't okay. It was her body, her responsibility, and he was the one scrambling to fix *her* mess.

For an instant he saw a ghostly image of himself lean over the toilet and drop the dispenser inside out of spite. It was a dumb thought: the dispenser was too big to flush away, and it would increase the chances of her actually staying pregnant.

"Staying . . ."

The thought jagged him like a mental paper cut. Was that how it worked? Did a girl get pregnant each time she had sex, and the job of the pill was to kill the fetus as it began to grow? Was that what they were doing? Making and killing babies at the same time?

He realized he was still gripping the birth-control dispenser and shoved it into his pocket with a quick motion. It felt better not to look at it. Connect the dots; one association led into another.

There were two bedroom doors facing each other in the hallway, both closed. The one on the left had a green, wooden M above the frame—Mandy's favorite color—which meant the other room had to belong to her roommate. He didn't know much about her. Less than a month ago a mutual friend had introduced them, and shortly thereafter, they had moved in together. Mandy was impetuous and stupid like that; always quick to trust. Who moved in with someone they just met?

He stared at the roommate's door. The girl was either gone for the night . . . or maybe just dead asleep in the bed. With all the noise he'd been making, she'd have to be out cold. He told himself to leave it alone. There was absolutely no reason to open the door and look inside. With his luck, she would walk through the front door the second he looked, and then what? *Sorry, just checking to see if you were home?*

"Tampons," he said under his breath. "Mandy's having her period and she needs tampons, and I was looking for some."

No reason at all to open the door . . . except that he wanted to. More than anything, he wanted to look inside. It wasn't like he was going to *do* anything. And if he did find someone asleep, he would simply back himself out and quietly shut the door.

He pressed his ear against the wood, listening for any signs of life. His hand went to the knob.

Maybe she sleeps in the nude, a voice whispered.

He gently opened the door. The light from the hallway spilled across the bed, revealing a crumpled, fluffy bedspread. No girl.

"Idiot," he told himself, but his heart was beating fast.

He flipped on the light. Concert posters were plastered across the walls, and a guitar with missing strings leaned against the dresser. He thought he remembered Mandy saying the girl was in some sort of garage band . . .

"Suzie," he said, pulling her name from memory.

He picked up the purple bra by his feet. The material was soft and silky, a far cry from the bland bras that Mandy wore. He carried it to the dresser and looked at the curled photographs tacked to her bulletin board. Near the bottom was a picture of Mandy and Suzie posing with beers in front of a pool. Mandy was in a drab one-piece swimsuit, while Suzie sported a yellow bikini. He wondered if Suzie would have any scruples about dating him if he broke it off with Mandy. All was fair in love and war, as they said. Or something like that.

The photo disappeared into his jacket pocket. He glanced at the clock; Mandy was probably fuming because he was taking so long. As if on cue, a telephone rang: a small, muffled sound from the other room. He took a final look around and killed the light.

"Yeah, yeah," he said petulantly, kicking open Mandy's door and searching for the light. "I'm on my way—"

His hand froze in the air. There had been a noise from the living room, almost like a faint *thump*.

He stood without moving until the phone cut off in mid-ring. Everything was quiet except for the beating of his heart.

Neighbors, that was all. The walls were thin and sound traveled easily.

The front doorknob shook.

It took Scott all of a half-second to process this information, and when the front door banged open, he snapped off the hallway light and slipped into Mandy's room.

"Damn thing always sticks," said a female voice.

He sneaked a peek around the doorway. Suzie he recognized immediately, but the other girl he didn't know. She was tall and skinny with dark hair that ended halfway down her back.

"Who was it again?" the girl asked. "Your cousin?"

"Yeah," Suzie answered. "Kelly had talked about getting her belly button pierced for years, but I never thought she'd actually go through with it."

Tall Girl dropped her purse on the couch and tossed a glance down the dark hallway. Scott shrank back and felt his heart and testicles meet somewhere in his stomach.

"Did they use a gun-thingy?" Tall Girl asked. "Like when they do your ears?"

"No, they used a curved needle the size of a pencil. I watched them push it through her skin."

Scott leaned forward as Suzie disappeared into the kitchen. Tall Girl was shaking her head.

"It was brutal," Suzie's voice drifted out. "But that part didn't bother my cousin at all. It was when the woman started talking about how fat cells will come out of the wound, and how it was real important to keep the wound clean. *That* was when Kelli started to faint."

"Really?" Tall Girl stepped into the kitchen and out of sight. "That's weird."

"I know, right? What was it that she said again . . ."

Scott's fingers curled around the edge of the door, drawing imaginary splinters. The conversation seemed to be on pause—long enough that he actually thought the two of them had disappeared through some invisible portal inside the kitchen.

Suzie finished: "She said it wasn't the *act* that bothered her; it was the recovery period."

A cupboard door closed, followed by running water. Scott pushed the door shut to a crack and looked around the room. He needed a plan and needed one fast. It wasn't like he could just stand there all night. The voice of reason told him to go out and announce himself—he did have permission to be there—but another stronger voice kept his shoes cemented to the floor. This voice said: *If you aren't hiding, then you should have gone out the second they walked inside.*

"Finish up those sandwiches," Suzie said. "I'm gonna grab some rippers for the party. My ass has been dragging all day and needs a good kick."

Scott's heart slowed to a crawl at the sound of approaching footsteps. There was an audible click and light spilled into the hallway from the other room.

"Mustard?" Tall Girl asked.

"Mayo," Suzie called back. "Lots of it."

Scott pushed his eye to the edge of the door and saw her standing by the bed, reaching to the shelf above her dresser. Her fingers fumbled with a small wooden box that was just out of reach. It fell to the ground and she cussed loudly enough to make Scott jump.

"Everything okay back there?" Tall Girl asked.

Suzie's knees popped as she crouched. "Just me being a klutz as always."

Scott nudged open the door a few inches, trying to see past the corner of the bed. His balance shifted, and before he could catch himself, his elbow struck the door with a thud. He stiffened and pressed himself up against the wall behind the door.

"Mandy? Is that you?"

Every inch of his body went tight. He could see Suzie in his mind's eye: looking toward the bedroom with a frown, trying to decide if she had really heard the sound. He stayed perfectly still. In a few seconds she would return to the kitchen, and a few minutes later they would leave the apartment—

The hallway light clicked. Mandy's bedroom door opened and crept to a stop just shy of his feet.

Nothing inside him moved—he even managed to stop the blood from pumping through his veins.

"What's up?" Tall Girl asked. "Mandy here?"

He could smell Suzie's perfume through the door and hear her shallow, rapid breathing. Now she would turn on the bedroom light, step inside, and see him hiding there. That was when she would scream.

"She's at work," Suzie said, but her voice didn't sound quite sure. "She works all night."

There was another long pause. A moment later the hallway went dark, and Scott forced himself to stay motionless as a cold wave of sweat flushed down his back. When he heard them back inside the kitchen, he let out his breath in one great shuddering sigh.

"We'll take the sandwiches with us," Suzie's voice drifted out. "We can eat in the car on the way over."

A cupboard door banged, followed by a clomping of footsteps, and—with a loud clap—the apartment door closed. Scott stuck his head into the hallway, half-expecting to see them standing there, pointing and saying *gotcha*! The only movement was the chain lock swinging from the doorframe like a pendulum.

The phone rang again. Scott wiped a hand across his mouth and snared the receiver from the wall. "Yeah, I'm on my way, okay?"

"You are?" asked a male voice. "You do house calls?"

Scott frowned. "Who's this?"

There was no response. In the background he could hear talking and laughing; it sounded like a party.

"Whatever," Scott said. "You got a wrong number—"

"I'm looking for Mandy."

His brow creased as everything registered: some guy was calling for his girlfriend. At one o'clock in the morning. "Who are you?"

"Are you Mandy's boyfriend?" the guy asked.

Scott's fingers tightened around the receiver. "Maybe. What is it to you?"

There was a chortle of laughter in the background.

"Dude, your girl has her name and number carved into a bathroom stall door down at Cline's Bar." And then in a mechanical voice: "This has been a public service announcement."

There was another riff of laughter and the line went dead. Scott stood there with the phone pressed against his ear, trying to process what had just happened. Mandy's name was scratched inside a bar bathroom, probably hooked to the words: *For a good time, call . . .*

For a moment he actually had a vague notion to chuckle as he visualized this joker collecting phone numbers from bathroom stall doors and then making calls with his buddies . . . but another part of his brain was already mulling over more serious business. It wasn't every day a girl earned a spot on a bathroom wall, and it was usually achieved by pissing off—or sleeping with—the wrong guy. He had no idea of Mandy's life before him, and it disturbed him to think of what she had done. He was banging a slut. A hole in the mattress. And if she was a joke, what did that make him?

"Nothing," he whispered.

He set the phone back into the cradle. The weight of it was incredibly heavy in his hand. He was tired—more tired than he had felt in his life. All he wanted to do was lie down and let himself slip away. He could feel his skin writhing and twisting, trying to crawl off and have a life of its own. To walk around and do whatever it wanted. Having nothing to think about or worry about. No consequences.

"Goddamn sleep," he told himself. "The mind cannot function properly without it. It wasn't meant to."

His attention went back to Suzie's room, back to the wooden box above the dresser. His legs carried him without a thought, and he removed the lid with little surprise. Inside were a handful of white pills. *My ass has been dragging,* Suzie's voice echoed inside his head, *and needs a good kick.* God knew *he* could use some kick.

He popped one of the pills into his mouth and began to suck. This way the drug would slowly be introduced into his system, and he could gauge its effect before taking more. He wasn't a total idiot. Pills could kill you. He put three more into his pocket and returned the box to its place on the shelf. If Suzie noticed any were missing, she would blame Mandy.

He made his way to the front door and lingered at the doorway, unsettled. Mandy's birth control was in his pocket, he had the apartment key . . . but something felt undone. Something was eating away at him, something that had been said. His mind struggled to unearth it: it was like trying to remember the name of an actor in a movie.

"The recovery period," he said aloud. "It wasn't the act that bothered her . . . it was the *recovery* period."

His mind clacked away at the words with the mental typewriter, straining to see what it looked like on paper. Things weren't worse after the fact—then it was over. The worst was while it was happening.

"Some people just don't get it," he said.

He left without bothering to lock the door behind him.

[22]

They sat without speaking as the Camaro idled in the Night Owl parking lot, each staring out their respective windows. There didn't seem to be much of anything to say as far as Kevin was concerned. And there would be no exchange of e-mails—he was sure of that.

"Thanks again," Sarah said.

"Sure." It was the third time she had thanked him, and he found himself wishing he had never picked her up. After everything that had happened—everything that had been said and done—it had come down to him being some dumb kid being led around by a pretty face.

"I should probably get going," he said, drumming his fingers against the steering wheel. "Gotta get up early. You know how it is."

She nodded but made no motion to leave. He could only imagine why she wasn't getting out of the car, or what she wanted from him now. He had nothing left to give. All he wanted was to get through this moment and tomorrow she would be a memory. He wasn't even sure he wanted to write about it anymore.

"Goodbye, Kevin."

He stiffened as she leaned over and kissed him on the cheek, and with a slam of the car door, she was gone. It was over. He realized he didn't even know her last name.

"Bye," he said in a hollow voice.

His hand went to his cheek as he looked at the hotel, wondering what she would do if her friend wasn't there. Not that it mattered. She wasn't his responsibility anymore. It was time to go home, peel off his clothing, and fall into a deep slumber for the next nine hours. Then he would be good again.

"Good as shit," he said and tried on a smile. It fell flat as he backed out of the parking lot. He could already imagine her laughing with her friend about the dork that had chauffeured her around all night. Scott was probably some successful business type. He probably didn't waste his time pounding on a keyboard and telling stories no one wanted to read. Only stupid kids with stupid dreams did that.

He spared a final glance at the hotel before stomping on the gas and leaving a small burst of smoke in the air.

• • •

Sarah ran back into the parking lot just as Kevin pulled onto the street. Her hands went into the air to wave him back, but it was too late—he was out of sight.

"Dammit, Sarah," she told herself.

She'd been hovering behind the lobby doors the entire time, listening to the Camaro's muffler and hoping he would come after her. That was dumb; she should have made him come inside with her. She couldn't let it end like this. It was impossible for it to end like this.

She re-entered the lobby and gave a weary nod to the girl behind the counter, who was watching with what looked to be mild trepidation. Not that Sarah blamed her; one minute she was cowering by the doors, and the next minute she was flying out of them like a crazed woman.

"Sorry about that," Sarah said.

"Do you need a room or something?" the girl asked. "You can't just hang around here for no reason."

"Sorry," Sarah said again, slightly flustered. "I'm looking for Scotty Mason. His brother Wade said that he might be here."

"Scott doesn't work here."

"Yes, I know . . . but is he here? Are you his girlfriend?"

The girl shrugged. "We screw on a regular basis."

"How wonderful for you. So is he here or not?"

"And who are you again?" the girl asked.

"Just . . . I'm an old friend."

"Like an old *girlfriend*?"

Sarah sighed. "He gave me a titty-twister when we were ten, but it was only on a dare. Does that count?"

"What does *that* mean?"

"Look," said Sarah, "it's been a craptacular night, and I've spent the last few hours trying to find Scotty. Can you help me or not?"

The girl's brow creased. "You don't have to get all pissy about it."

"You know what? Forget it." Sarah slung her purse on the counter and dug for her credit card. "Just give me a room."

"Well, he might be back in a minute," the girl said. "Maybe he just ran an errand—"

"Don't care." Sarah tossed the card on the counter. "One single for one night."

The girl stared at the card without moving.

"Is there a problem?" Sarah asked. "This is a hotel, right? I'd like a single room for a single night."

The girl snatched up the card and replaced it with a registration slip. "Smoking?"

"I quit."

"How wonderful for you."

Sarah clenched her teeth as she scratched out her information. She pushed the registration card back and kept one eye on the credit card as the girl ran it through the machine. The card was for emergencies and had never been used; she wasn't even sure she had called the number to activate it. If not, it was going to be a long night. She had cash, but not enough for a room or a cab ride home.

"Guess it's not stolen after all," the girl said. She dropped the card on the counter along with a key card. "Room 123."

"Thanks," Sarah said, grabbing the items. "You've been a real treat."

Sarah hurried off around the corner . . . but not before hearing a final word from the girl's mouth: *skank*.

[23]

It took a series of wrong turns before Sarah found her room, and at that point she wasn't optimistic the key card would work. The girl had probably neglected to code it, just out of spite.

The lock flashed green when she swiped the card, and she pushed open the door with an exhale of relief. The inside of a hotel room had never looked so good. She dropped onto the bed, face first. All she wanted to do was lie there and forget about Kevin, Scotty, and her mother . . . who was probably worried to death about her. Probably sitting by the door . . . crying her eyes out . . . picking up the phone every few seconds to make sure it was still working . . .

"Okay," she told herself. "I'll call."

She dialed home. The phone began to ring. And ring. And ring.

"So much for being worried sick," she mumbled.

The answering machine clicked on to let her know that the Cates were unavailable and to leave a name and number after the beep.

"Hi, Mom, I wanted to let you know I'm fine. I'm staying at the Night Owl Hotel in Duncerton. I'm with Scotty Mason and everything's okay. And I'm . . . sorry about earlier. We'll talk more tomorrow."

She hung up and replayed the message in her head. Meeting Scotty was probably a long shot at this point, but she figured it would make her mother feel better. Scotty was an old friend of the family, after all.

She kicked off her sandals and went into the bathroom. The thought of a hot shower was too inviting to pass up, and she was grateful to find a stack of fresh towels inside. The last thing she wanted to do was call the girl at the front desk for anything.

"She's Scotty's girlfriend," she told herself. "There must be something good about her."

But that wasn't necessarily true. She hardly knew Scotty anymore, and the last time they had spoken was at his father's funeral. Before that, she couldn't remember the last time they had talked. Six months? A year? They had so much history together that she still believed he would be there for her in a jam.

"Probably," she said. "Maybe."

The truth of the matter was that she didn't know anything anymore. She was in a strange hotel in a strange town, and it was a cold, bitter world that was more than happy to chew you up and spit you out. The whole evening had been proof of that.

She shut the bathroom door behind her and started the shower. "Single, alone, and soon to be naked. Couldn't ask for a better birthday."

She peeled off her shirt and frowned at her reflection in the mirror. She really was single again. Single and free to do nothing with nobody. And was it really that big of a shock? As many times as she had been hit on in her life, she could still never understand the attraction. Her breasts were small, her hair did a funny cowlick thing that made it almost impossible to work with, and her eyes were too big for her head, making her look like one of those Japanese cartoon character girls. She also looked young for her age and wondered if that was an attraction.

Kevin the kid, a voice whispered . . . and she tried not to think about it as she touched the bruise on her forehead. Kevin was for tomorrow. Somehow she would find him, even if she had to knock on every single door in town.

She pulled off her remaining clothes, climbed into the shower, and stayed inside until her fingers were wrinkled and pink. When she stepped out, she carefully wrapped a towel around her body and hair, and left the bathroom in a complete state of relaxation.

"Hi, Sarah."

She let out a scream. Scotty was sitting on the edge of the bed with his head tilted to one side. A greasy length of hair hung over his bloodshot eyes, and his face was hollow and gaunt.

"How did you get in here?" she choked, holding the towel in place with both hands.

"Mandy told me where you were. I knocked a bunch of times but you never answered. I was worried something was wrong, so I persuaded her to give me a master key card. When I got in here, I heard the shower running, so I figured I'd just wait." He smiled at her. "It's really good to see you, Sarah. Really good."

There was a knock on the door, and Sarah felt her heart and breath stop simultaneously.

"That's probably Mandy," Scott said. "She wasn't too happy about me wanting to see you, and she probably thinks we're in here doing the nasty. She's jealous like that. She also didn't like you very much. I'll answer it."

He stood and went for the door. Sarah was halfway back into the bathroom when she heard: "Is Sarah here? The girl at the counter told me this was her room . . ."

Kevin was standing in the doorway. Sarah didn't know whether to laugh or cry.

<h1 style="text-align:center">THREE</h1>

The four of them all but filled the small lobby: Mandy behind the counter, Scotty leaning against it, and Kevin and Sarah sitting in the chairs. Scotty was acting perfectly normal, droning on while tossing grins in everyone's direction.

"So I've been living with my brother Wade for the last month," he said, "looking for a job and all that. My dipshit roommate is holding my stuff captive until I can give him the rent I owe. Which ain't gonna happen."

Sarah sneaked a glance at Kevin. He hadn't said why he had come back, and she didn't dare try to make a guess. She was running on faith again.

"I can't believe I never mentioned Sarah before," Scott said, looking at Mandy over his shoulder. "I was sure I did."

"No," Mandy replied tonelessly.

"My bad. But this is really great, the four of us here. Really super. Sorry you had so much trouble finding me,

Sarah. I would have been more than happy to let you crash at my place if I had one."

For that she was gladder than she would ever let anyone know. Not his offer to let her stay, but the fact that he *had* no place to offer. All she wanted now was to talk to Kevin alone. The problem was finding an opening to escape into.

"So how long have you two been going out?" Scott asked, pointing at Kevin. "You're Matt, right?"

"Kevin," Kevin answered stiffly.

Scott rolled his finger to Sarah. "I thought you and some guy named Matt were hitting the sheets. Wade saw your mother a few weeks ago and she said she thought she might have a new son-in-law soon. What's up with that?"

"I should go," Kevin said, pushing himself out of the chair.

"We need to talk," Sarah said. She grabbed Kevin by the arm and led him down the hallway.

"It's pretty late, Sarah. I just came back because I found your comb on the floor of my car. You must have dropped it earlier when you were looking through your purse."

"You're not leaving until I say a few things," she said, surprised at the harshness of her voice. She pushed open the doors that led into the recreation area and led him to the chairs by the pool. "Put your butt right there, Kevin. Sit there and *listen*."

He only held out the comb. "Do you want this or not?"

She grabbed it and tossed it away, shifting her weight too quickly. Her left sandal slipped out from under her, and the next second there was an explosion of water and everything went dark. Her feet found the floor of the pool and she pushed her head up through the surface, spitting out a mouthful of water and sucking in a breath.

"Are you okay?" Kevin cried.

He was kneeling by the edge of the pool with his jaw unhinged; he looked like one of those clown faces you shot in the mouth at the carnival to win a prize. She began to giggle and then to laugh. He gave her a cocked eyebrow.

"*Now* do you want the comb?" he asked.

She burst into laughter, and all at once his face broke and he was laughing alongside her. It was the most glorious sound she had heard all night.

[24]

He had watched the entire scene unfold from the second floor balcony—they hadn't known he was there. After she had fallen into the pool, they had gone back into room 123, undoubtedly to strip off their clothes and get down to business. He didn't know anything about the kid, but he knew the kid's name. That would have to do for now. The rest wasn't important. What was important was that he knew where they were, and he could keep an eye on them. She wasn't going to treat him like common dirt—not after everything they had been through together. They had history, and he wasn't going to let her throw that away.

He would wait until the light inside the room went off—all night if he had to.

He wanted to catch them in the act.

[25]

Mandy glowered as Scott came back into the lobby. His hands were shoved into the pockets of his jeans jacket, and his face was cut into a grimace. He stalked past her and looked out into the parking lot.

"Where did you run off to?" she asked.

"None of your business." His fists opened and closed as he paced the floor. "Nowhere."

"I don't want you to see her again," Mandy told him. "Do you hear me? I don't like her, and I'm two seconds away from kicking her ass out of here. Don't think I won't. I can call the general manager and tell him she's causing a disturbance, and he'll give me permission to call the cops. I've done it before."

"Shut your mouth," Scott said under his breath.

Mandy slammed down her notebook. "What did you just say? Scott Mason, I have half a mind to—"

"To *what*?" he yelled. "Leave me? Walk out on me like everyone else has?"

He whirled and punched the wall with a shout, which immediately morphed into a yowl of pain. He staggered sideways and dropped into the chair, cradling his injured hand.

"Are you crazy?" Mandy rasped, gaping at the damage to the wall. "You can't punch holes in the place where I work. You're going to get me in trouble."

"It was an accident," he said. He flexed his fingers and was surprised to find the pain was already smoothing to a dull ache. "You're right. I shouldn't have done it. It was wrong of me. Can you get me a cigarette?"

She only looked at him.

"Please. I need something to help kill the pain."

"This is what I'm saying, Scott," she said. "This is so messed up. One minute you act like you want to kill someone, and then the next minute you're all *normal* like nothing just happened."

"You're right. I think something is broken inside me. I thought about what you said. Something is wrong. I just get . . . confused sometimes. Sometimes it feels like I'm not myself. I need help. I'm going to get help. But right now . . . right now I need a smoke. And you can help me by giving me that smoke. Will you please help me, Mandy?"

"Whatever." She grabbed the cigarettes and shoved them into his hands. "Here."

"Thank you," he said. "Thank you, Mandy. You're too good to me. You really are. Please don't call the manager. I won't go see Sarah again. I swear. She's had a hard life. Let's just leave her and her boyfriend in peace for tonight. Okay?"

Mandy crossed her arms. "What's the story with her? Did you guys *date* or something?"

"We grew up together. She had a thing for me a while ago, but I never felt that way about her. She's like my sister. Seeing her has brought up a lot of old memories—some not so good. It's messing with my head. But you're right. It's best not to talk to her or see her again. You're absolutely right."

"She's not even that pretty," Mandy said with a pout. "Maybe *some* guys like girls with stringy hair and dark skin, but not classy guys."

"You're absolutely right," he said again. "Don't give her another thought. She's not worth the time. And after tonight she'll be gone forever, and we'll never have to think or worry about her again."

"What does that mean? After tonight she'll be gone *forever*?"

Scott wiped the back of his mouth with his hand. "She'll be gone in the morning when she checks out. Checkout is at eleven, yeah?"

"Yeah . . ."

"She'll check out of the hotel, leave to go back home, and I'll probably never see her again. She'll be gone from us forever."

"I guess. It was just the way you said it—"

"I think I should go to the bathroom and run some cold water over my hand. I'll be back. You sit tight. Don't worry about me, Mandy. I'm fine. Everything is fine."

He stumbled past her into the hallway. When he found his way back into the bathroom, it was only a matter of seconds before he was on his knees over the toilet again.

[26]

Just great, Sarah thought, hovering over the mound of wet clothing piled inside the bathtub. A sense of déjà vu washed over her, only this time when she stepped out of the bathroom in her towel, it would be Kevin—not Scotty—sitting on the bed. She assumed there was a laundry somewhere in the hotel, but for now, the clothes would have to wait. The last thing she wanted was for Kevin to run off again.

She fidgeted with her hair in the mirror, trying desperately to get it to do something with no luck. At least her hair wasn't as bad as her new eyeliner—two dark bags hanging under her lids. She tightened the towel around her body, bit her lip, and opened the bathroom door.

"I should go," Kevin said.

"Sit," she commanded, pointing to the bed. "I'm sure you've seen a girl in a towel before."

The new attitude of hers was scaring and exciting her. She had never been a take-charge girl before, but she suspected there were going to be a lot of changes after this night. Changes for the better.

"I can run out and get you some clothes from my trunk," he offered. "It's my stuff, so I know it would fit you. It'd just be a little big."

"That's okay," she told him. "I'll probably just hang my clothes up to dry on the shower rod." She almost added: *I sleep in the nude anyway, so it's okay*, but decided against it. It sounded slutty. It also wasn't true.

She sat down on the bed and did a quick check to make sure none of her lower package was peeking out. She knew it was stupid, but a small part of her was excited. She didn't know if she thought something was going to happen . . . or even if she *wanted* something to happen . . . it was all messed up in her head. All she knew was that she once again felt right with him there. She felt safe. She tried to imagine his face if she were to stand up and accidentally drop the towel to the floor. It was all harmless flirting.

Sitting half-naked in a hotel room with a guy is hardly harmless flirting, a voice inside her seared. *It is very serious business.*

"Maybe some other clothes would be good," she said. "Thank you."

"Back in one minute."

She let out a sigh after the door shut and lay back on the bed. The towel slipped free and dropped around her body, exposing her fully to the ceiling.

Please have forgotten your car keys or something, she thought half-jokingly. *I'll just lie here and close my eyes and hope for the best.*

Only one guy had ever seen her naked, and that had been the only guy she had ever slept with. An hour after it was over he had turned into a jerk, and less than twenty-four hours later he had dumped her. That had been her introduction to the asshole boyfriends of the world, and it had been a hell of an initiation.

"So I need a second chance to make up my mind," she said, standing and facing the door. She propped her hand against the wall and puckered her lips. When Kevin came back she would march right up to him, lock her arms around his waist, and commence with the steamiest make-out session this room had ever witnessed.

"Come on in, Kevin," she whispered. She bounced her hips and raised her eyebrows seductively. "You have seen a naked girl before, haven't you, *Kevin*?"

There was a knock on the door. She snatched the towel from the bed, quickly re-fastened it around her body, and let him in.

"Sweat pants and a T-shirt," he said. "Hope they'll do."

She took them and blushed as their hands touched. "Don't go anywhere."

He nodded as she returned to the bathroom and closed the door. She could hear him moving around the room, and she felt a trickle of excitement as she removed her towel. The only thing separating them was a flimsy hollow door.

Just get dressed, she scolded herself.

Kevin was sitting in the chair when she came back out, and a grin tipped one corner of his mouth.

"Something funny?" she asked, trying to sound threatening.

"Nope. Only that my clothing looks *way* better on you than it does me."

"And tell me again why you carry around clothes in your car?"

"In case someone falls into a pool," he said matter-of-factly. "Why else? Hey, I'm going to go grab something to drink. Do you want me to bring you back anything?"

"I'll come with you."

She followed him out the door and toward the vending machines. A small noise caught her ear and she cast a glance over her shoulder. All at once she felt jumpy, and she knew it was because of Scotty. Part of her wished she wasn't in the same town as him, let alone the same hotel.

"I'm a sucker for orange juice," Kevin said, sorting through the coins in his palm. "What do you want? I have plenty of change."

"I'm good. Maybe I can just have a drink of yours?"

"Sure."

She lifted her head; there had been a flicker of movement on the walkway above them—she was sure of it.

She flinched when the orange juice bottle came rattling down the chute.

"Is this okay?" he asked.

"Yeah," she said absently. "Orange juice is fine."

"No. I mean . . . is it okay that I'm here? Is it okay that I came back?"

Her pulse shifted to a higher gear as her eyes found his. Everything else around her was immediately forgotten. "Yes. I'm glad you came back."

"Because I wanted to tell you . . . that is . . . I've never been good at *talking* about my feelings. And back at the bar . . . I'm sorry about the way I was. I just couldn't . . ."

He was staring past her, not meeting her eyes.

"It's one of the reasons I write," he said. "It's so much easier to express myself through stories. And lots of times I feel like it's the only time I control my world. I decide what happens. I can get it all out on paper, and people will never know if it's true or not. But I don't have paper to hide behind right now . . ."

She looked at him carefully as he spoke. His gaze was trained on the bottle in his hands.

"I . . . *like* you, Sarah." The words seemed to be cutting his lips as they came out. "I have no right to put you on the spot like this, especially since you have a boyfriend. I came back because I wanted to see you again. I wanted to talk to you. But if you don't want me here, just tell me and I'll go. I don't want to be a nuisance."

"Nuisance? After everything you've done for me tonight? How can you think that?"

"Last month, I asked my father for a new mattress because mine was so worn it was starting to come apart at the seams. When I got home the next day, the entire bed was gone, and in its place was a sleeping bag that smelled like piss. I'm pretty sure he found it in a dumpster. He told me it was my birthday present."

Sarah cupped a hand over her mouth. "Are you joking?"

"I don't want to be a nuisance," he said again.

Her hands latched on to his shoulders. She didn't care what he thought about the gesture or even if he returned it.

"Don't go," she whispered. "Kevin . . ."

You'll be safe with me, she finished to herself. *We'll be safe in each other.*

[27]

Scott held the picture in his hands, staring at it without blinking. He knew every color and every wrinkle in the photo paper. Just looking at it could almost whisk him back to the day it was taken. The two of them were sitting at the kitchen table, arms draped around each other, their tongues stuck out for the camera.

"Scott?"

The picture slipped from his hands and floated to the floor. He snatched it up and closed his fist around it.

"What's that?" Mandy asked, leaning over the counter. Scott hadn't heard her come out from the back room. "Who is it?"

"Me and my mom," he said. "I'm still not feeling too good. I think I'm going to lie down by the pool in one of the loungers. Maybe try to get some sleep."

"Whatever. Just don't bother any of the guests, especially your girlfriend in room 123. If she's still alive."

"Why do you say that?" Scott asked.

"No reason."

He grabbed her wrist. Hard.

"Scott, that hurts—"

"What do you mean?" he hissed.

Mandy wriggled in his grip, unable to get loose. "I'll tell you; just let go!"

She jerked away as he released her. There was a red imprint of his fingers around her wrist. "You don't have to abuse me."

"Tell me," he said.

"It's nothing," she said with a pout. "It happened last year before you and I were together. In room 123. One of the housekeepers found someone dead in there."

"Dead?"

"Some guy. He was lying in the bathtub with his head bashed in. They said it looked like he was beaten with a baseball bat or something."

"You're making this up."

"I'm serious," she replied peevishly. "It was all over the news. They said it was just probably a random crime or something."

"And you put her in that room because of that?"

She gave him a dry smile. "Sometimes history repeats itself."

He marched away in disgust, cramming the picture of him and Sarah back into his wallet.

"Sarah, why did you come here?" he whispered.

After all these months of not seeing or hearing from her, why show up now? It had nothing to do with needing to spend the night somewhere—she wanted something from him. It was obvious that the kid had some kind of hold over her, and until he got her alone, he wouldn't be able to talk to her in any sort of meaningful way.

Room 123 was just down to the left, and he slowed his step as his heart began to race.

What are you thinking, Scott? a voice warned. To his disgust it sounded like Mandy. Mandy inside his head—that was true horror.

He stopped in front of room 121 and pressed his ear to the door. There were no sounds from inside, and he slipped the master key card into the lock. The door popped open, and he stiffened when he saw people asleep in the beds. A little girl with red hair sat up and looked at him with wide eyes. He pressed a finger to his lips, and she clamped two tiny hands over her mouth and giggled. She leaned forward as he closed the door, watching him through the crack as it narrowed until it was shut.

He lingered for a moment to catch his balance before creeping past room 123 and sliding the key card into room 125.

This time he discovered what he wanted: the room was empty. He tossed an almost indifferent glance over his shoulder to see if anyone was around . . . and froze. On the other side of the pool area he saw a face in the window of a hallway door.

And then it was gone.

He hurried into the room and chain locked the door behind him. After a second he lifted the curtain and peeked out the window. The pool area was deserted, no sign of anything or anyone.

"Mind games," he said, calming himself with long, deep breaths. Another side effect of the insomnia. His eyes were screwing with him; that was all.

He shed his jacket and stumbled into the bathroom. He was genuinely surprised by how horrible he looked in the mirror; he really didn't feel that awful anymore. He splashed his face with cold water and dug Suzie's pills from his pocket. The first dose had taken off some of the edge, but now he was ready for the main event.

He swallowed the remaining pills using water from his cupped hands, already feeling better. Now all he had to do was to wait for the kid to leave again. Then he would have his chance. His chance to make everything right.

He moved to the corner, sat on the floor, and pressed his ear against the wall that connected with room 123.

[28]

"You sure you want to hear this?" Kevin asked.

"Yes."

He was sitting in the chair in the corner of the room. Sarah was on the bed. The orange juice was gone, but he still had the bottle in his hands, twisting the cap off and on.

"I was sixteen," he said, speaking in a low voice. "It was summer, and I was out with some buddies, causing trouble as always. You know how small towns are. There's really nothing *to* do but get into trouble. In junior high I was into stuff like toilet-papering houses, cutting down rural speed limit signs, and spray-painting walls. By the time I had turned sixteen, I had graduated to stealing from stores, smashing windshields on cars, and picking fights with anyone who looked at me funny."

Sarah opened her mouth in protest; she couldn't believe this guy was capable of inflicting pain on others. Her mind went back to the fight at the bar and she said nothing.

"Do you remember when the head of the town statue was stolen a few years back?" he asked.

"Yeah," she exclaimed, "the head was sawed off . . ."

"Jeremiah and me," he said with a mirthless smile. "We threw the head into the river and watched it sink. I remember looking down into the muddy water and thinking I would just jump in after it . . . wondering if I would sink down to the bottom with it. Half of the vandalism you read about in the paper over the last few years could probably be blamed on my friends and me.

"Like I said, it was summer. I was down at the bus terminal with my buddies Chad, Rik, and Steve. It was a simple idea: pick a poor sucker getting off the bus and throw shit at him. And I literally mean *shit*, as in animal feces. Steve lived near a farm and it was easy enough to fill a bucket."

Sarah felt her stomach do a small flip. "Good to know."

"So there we were, hidden off to the side of the terminal, watching the people trickle off the bus. All we needed was the right person. And since I was the one that thought it up, the guys were waiting for me to pick. I must have watched a dozen people get off that bus, but none of them felt right. It was mostly old people or parents with kids. I didn't want to give anyone a heart attack or traumatize some kid for life . . . I wanted someone who could take it. Someone who would get pissed off and maybe come after us. Like I said, I wanted to fight. I always wanted to fight."

He shook his head.

"Just as I was about to settle on a middle-aged guy who almost looked homeless, one last guy steps off the bus. The guy looked to weigh maybe three hundred pounds, but he was built hard, not fat. He looked like a motorcycle biker, like my father used to be. I told my buddies this was the one. They all began to freak because the guy was so big, but I didn't care. All I could think about was my father, the asshole he was, and how this guy reminded me of him. And the guy was playing the victim perfectly. Just standing there by the street lamp with his bag at his feet, looking at a piece of paper he had taken from his back pocket. He was just *waiting* for it."

Sarah flinched a little as Kevin shifted in the chair. He was all keyed up—his eyes were tiny slits.

"I think the other guys took off running before the shit left my hand, but I didn't care. I was watching the guy. I wanted to see his face.

"It nailed him in the shoulder and cheek, and he immediately turned and saw me. But the funny thing was, his expression didn't change. He didn't look mad or pissed off . . . he just stood there, staring at me, and I stood there looking back at him. It was only when a couple of people around him began shouting and pointing in my direction that I got out of there. People knew me in town, and I knew I was probably busted. But I didn't care. I didn't care at all.

"I made my way home alone, pissed off at the guys for deserting me. They were all a bunch of assholes as far as I was concerned. I figured to see them cowering outside my house when I got back home, but they weren't. There was only my father, sitting inside on the couch.

"I sat across from him, waiting for him to say that the police had been by, or that my friends had come around looking for me, but he only glared into the television like always. When I got up to go into my room he told me to fetch him a beer. I was halfway to the fridge when someone knocked on the door. My father shouted at me to answer it, and I did as I was told, bracing myself to see the cops. And when I pulled open the door, I nearly crapped my pants.

"It was the guy from the bus terminal. His face had been wiped clean, but there was still a wet spot on his shoulder. And I could still smell the manure on him.

"'Who is it?' my father asked.

"The guy and I stared at each other for what felt like forever. Up close he looked even worse. His skin was like old leather, and his eyes were cold and empty.

"'Who the hell is it?' my father asked again, looking over to see what was happening. His mouth dropped as I stumbled away from the door.

"'Son of a whore!' my father said with a laugh, struggling out of his chair. 'Harry, you old shitcracker, what are ya doing here?'

"I knew I was dead. And I'm not speaking metaphorically—I'm speaking literally. I knew I wasn't going to survive this.

"'I sent a letter a while back,' the guy said. 'Came in to town to visit my sister. Letter must have not made it.' He nodded in my direction. 'This your son?'

"'Yeah, this worthless piece of shit belongs to me. Don't pay him any mind.'

"The guy looked me up and down. I don't exactly know how long it was before he spoke, but it was the longest moment of my life.

"'That's one helluva shiner you got,' was what he said to me. 'I hope you made the other guy work for it.'

"I could feel my father watching me, daring me to speak. I said nothing. I only stood there, waiting for it to be over. And when the guy finally did move toward me, I stood my ground the best that I could . . . and almost lost my balance when he clapped me on the shoulder.

"'He looks like a good kid,' the guy said. 'I know a piece of shit when I see one. As long as he stays out of trouble, he'll be fine. We don't want him to end up like us.'

"My father grunted and whapped me in the stomach.

"'Don't just stand there. Get this guy a beer. Hey, you wanna use the shower, man? You kinda stink.'"

Kevin leaned back in the chair and blew a breath into his trembling hands. He wiped them across his jeans and cleared his throat.

"The guy stayed for dinner and never once brought up the incident. And before he left, he shook my hand when my father was out of earshot and said, 'Be good, kid. Some of us don't get a freebie.'"

Kevin stared past her with a frown.

"I don't know why the guy didn't say anything. Maybe he knew my father well enough to know what would happen. Why the guy even cared was beyond me. When I asked my father about him, he only said that they were once as close as brothers, but the guy had gone soft after getting out of jail. He didn't say why the guy had been to jail, and I didn't ask. All I knew was that I was off the hook, free to go back to doing what I wanted. But something inside me had changed. I don't know how to describe it exactly . . . it was as though something that was broken was suddenly fixed. After that, I drifted away from all my old friends. I saw myself becoming my father, and it scared the shit out of me. And I have some strange biker guy to thank for it, some guy that my father knew years ago. I know it doesn't make much sense . . . I can't explain it any better than that."

"You weren't kidding earlier," Sarah said. "When you said that you try to do one nice thing a day for someone, you really meant it."

"I did break one promise to myself tonight. I swore I would never fight again, but I had no choice. Those guys outside the bar . . . they never had a chance."

He said it without cockiness, just as matter-of-fact.

"The bruise on your stomach?" Sarah asked softly.

"I stayed out late last weekend and accidentally woke him when I came into the house."

He slouched in the chair. Sarah stared at him, a giant knot pulling at her own stomach. More than anything she wanted to pull him over to the bed and just put her arms around him. She opened her mouth and he stood.

"Let me find a dryer for your clothes," he said. He held up the empty orange juice bottle. "And I need another drink. Can I get you anything? Anything at all? I can go and find a gas station if you need me to."

She found herself at a loss. One minute he was telling her about his abusive father, and the next minute he was trying to take care of her.

"I really could use something else to drink," he said again without meeting her eyes.

She told herself to let him go. He looked extremely uncomfortable standing there, and there was entirely too much emotion in the room.

"You still owe me a sip," she finally answered. "Hold on; let me get the clothes."

She went into the bathroom and sighed at the wet mess in the bathtub. He was going to be carrying her bra and panties, and she wondered if he would sneak a peek at them to see what they looked like.

"Stuff it," she told herself firmly.

She wrapped her clothing in a fresh towel and carried them out. "You're coming back, right?"

He smiled. "I couldn't leave without my favorite sweat pants."

He went out the door and she sat back on the bed with a huff, a troubled frown etched into her lips.

She had a very bad feeling.

[29]

Scott looked over his shoulder as he stood at the soda machine, unable to shake the feeling of being watched. Standing out in the open made him feel vulnerable and exposed, but he needed a quick drink to fix his dry throat and fuzzy head. Lack of sleep and pills could do that to a person: make them fuzzy.

"Come on," he said, shoving the coins in faster than the machine would accept them. Every other quarter was dropping back down the return slot, and he tried to steady his hand as he scooped them back out. "Eat the damn money—"

A door slammed, giving him a start, and he caught sight of the kid leaving Sarah's room carrying an armful of towels. He shrank back behind the machine until the kid was out of sight, then bee-lined for Sarah's door. This was his chance to talk to her alone, and he wasn't about to miss it.

The curtains to her room were pulled tight. He knocked on the window and tried to peer inside. He went to the door and knocked again, making sure she could see him through the peephole. He served up his best smile as the door inched open, and his smile faltered when he saw she had on the chain lock.

"What do you want, Scotty?" she asked through the opening.

Not exactly the reaction he had hoped for, but she was confused and unsure of what she was saying. This was the kid talking—not her—clouding her mind with who knew what?

"Are you okay?" Scott asked.

"I'm fine."

"I wanted to make sure you were okay. And I wanted to tell you that my brother and his wife are leaving in the morning and they'll be gone for a week. If you still need somewhere to stay you can come over, Sarah. We can stay there. We'd have the place to ourselves. We could watch movies and talk all night, like we used to do."

"I just needed someplace for tonight," she said.

He placed his hand on the door. "Sarah, it's me, Scotty. Talk to me."

"Please, just go. I'll . . . call you later or something. I'll talk to you then."

"Sarah," he pleaded. He squeezed his fingers through the crack, just to show her that he was okay, and she moved back.

"It's this guy," Scott said angrily, "isn't it? This guy you're with. That's the reason you're being like this. What do you want me to do? All I want to do is help. You tell me what you want."

"I want you to just go," Sarah said. "You're weirding me out, Scotty."

She closed the door. Scott geared up to knock again and saw the kid—Kevin—walking past. The kid didn't stop, didn't speak, but his eyes never left Scott's. Scott followed him to the soda machine.

"You and Sarah having a good time in there?" Scott asked.

Kevin said nothing and began to feed change into the machine.

"Sarah and I go *way* back," Scott said. "She tell you that? We used to be best friends growing up. There is nothing I wouldn't do for her. Nothing."

Kevin smacked the orange juice button and collected the bottle.

"How long have you been dating?" Scott asked.

"We're not dating."

"So you're not her boyfriend, but you're here in a hotel room with her? That seems kind of messed up."

"It's a long story."

"You screwing her?" Scott asked.

"You know, all night when we were looking for you, I thought you must be some great guy . . . some *great* friend for her to go to so much trouble—"

"I'm not afraid of you," Scott said, his hand going into his pocket. "You don't scare me."

Kevin gave him a mechanical smile. "It was great meeting you."

"Ask Sarah about Jason Figman," Scott shouted after him. "Tell her not to forget who her *real* friends are."

Scott watched as the kid knocked on the door, then disappeared into the room with Sarah. *His* Sarah. Where *he* should be right now.

His hands curled into fists and the nails cut into his palms.

He welcomed the pain.

[30]

"Front desk," Mandy answered.

She listened patiently and told the woman that the problem would be taken care of.

"Dammit," she cussed, slamming down the phone. "Scott, you are a dead man."

She tromped out from behind the counter and marched down the hallway. The call had come from room 156, regarding a suspicious-looking man that had been hanging out around the pool area. Apparently this guy had been sneaking around for a while now, ducking in and out of hallways and trying to stay out of sight.

She burst through the doors into the pool area and fought down her anger as she surveyed the scene. A few of the rooms still had lights on, but most were dark. There was no sign of anyone.

"Scott!" she said in a loud whisper.

There was a noise to her left, and an elbow disappeared behind a clump of video games.

"Go home," she hissed. "Get out of here before you get me in trouble."

She could see his shape through the gap of two pinball machines. She took a step forward and heard a small tapping sound. It sounded like metal on metal. She stopped and the sound stopped.

"I don't know what game you're playing, Scott, but just *go*."

Silence.

The hairs on the back of her neck stirred as she took another small step and the sound began again—louder this time.

"Scott?" she whispered.

The sound fell quiet and was replaced by a voice talking very softly and very quickly. She couldn't make out anything it was saying, but it didn't sound like Scott. It didn't sound like Scott at all.

She traced her steps back to the hallway, tossing small glances over her shoulder, a chill following her all the way back to the counter.

[31]

Sarah drank half the orange juice in one gulp and gave Kevin
an embarrassed smile. "I guess I was thirstier than I realized.
Sorry."

"I talked to your friend," Kevin said. "He was out by the
vending machines."

"What did he say?"

"He told me to ask you about Jason Figman."

Sarah didn't answer right away, and after a moment she
stood and pulled at the blankets on the bed.

"Sarah, it's really late and if you want to sleep—"

"No," she said, shaking her head. "No, I'm just cold. Do
you mind if I get under? Please, don't leave. Please?"

He nodded. "Okay."

"Jason was a guy from high school. He was Scotty's
friend. One night the three of us were over at Scotty's house,
and when Scotty left the room to go get something, Jason
started wrestling with me. I told him to stop it, and he just
laughed. Then he started to grope me and I got scared. He

was laughing and pretending to wrestle, but his hands were all over me . . ."

She sighed.

Kevin asked softly, "Scotty?"

"Yeah," she said. "Scotty came in and pulled him off. I sat on the floor and watched the two of them go at it. Scotty basically kicked him a few times and punched him in the stomach. It was all very surreal. It was shortly after that when Scotty and I dated for a brief period. I felt such gratitude toward him for saving me . . . maybe that guy was going to rape me . . ."

She began to shake her head again.

"But it didn't make sense?" Kevin offered.

"Why would this Jason guy try this when Scotty was in the house and only gone for a few minutes? And when they were fighting . . . it didn't look like Jason was even trying."

"Scotty the hero," Kevin said. "Saving the day."

"After a couple weeks of dating I told Scotty it was too weird. Like I said, at the time it felt like he had saved me, but then again at the same time . . . about a week after that, Jason and Scotty were friends again. Scotty told me that it was all just a misunderstanding."

She shivered and drew the blanket to her chin.

"It doesn't really matter now," she said. "I feel so bad for Scotty. He's had such a tough time. Dad dead, doesn't talk to his mom . . . he's never really gotten a break for anything. He didn't even finish high school. They kicked him out for missing so much."

"Sounds like a rough time," Kevin said without sarcasm.

"The truth is, the Scotty I knew and loved as a friend disappeared a long time ago. It's funny how you can perceive people and build illusions around them. Maybe I didn't want to give up on him. Maybe that's why I sought him out tonight. And maybe he did save me that night."

She fell quiet as Kevin stared into the floor.

"Kevin?"

"Yeah?"

"Remember when you picked me up tonight? The first time on Kuennen Road, and I said I was with my boyfriend?"

He nodded.

"That was Matt."

"Why wasn't he walking with you?" Kevin asked.

"He stayed at the car. We had an argument. It was bad. He was probably passed out in the back seat when you drove by. I don't know if he's still there or at home now. I don't care."

"Oh."

"Can I ask you something?"

He nodded. "Anything."

"Why do you carry your clothes around in the trunk of your car?"

Kevin leaned forward. "Stay or go. That's the million-dollar question. High school is over. There's no money for me to go to college. I know people can get loans, but I can't imagine going thousands of dollars into debt for school. Not right now, anyway. If I stay in town, I'll probably end up working at the factory until I can scrape together enough money to afford my own place, which would probably be nothing more than a shitty trailer on the bad side of town. But that's not the worst part. The worst part is that this town is all I've ever known, and the thought of leaving it scares the shit out of me. For better or worse, it's been my whole world. So I made myself a deal. If I had a reason to leave, I'd take it. One reason. *Any* reason."

He reached into his pocket and pulled out an envelope. It was folded in half and wrinkled.

"What's that?" she asked timidly.

"I want to apologize for getting upset earlier when you called me a kid."

"Kevin, I—"

"When I submit my stories to the websites I was telling you about, you're supposed to also include a synopsis of your story, any previous publishing credits, and a brief biography of yourself."

"Okay . . ."

"To date, I have a total of forty-eight rejections and only one acceptance. In my defense, those forty-eight rejections are for *all* the stories I've written and submitted, not just a single story."

"Is that good or bad?"

He tried to smile. "Let's just say that after a while it gets depressing to be constantly rejected. It makes you wonder why you bother. Makes you wonder if you're good enough. If you're not just wasting your time and life."

"But you said earlier that one of your stories was going to be published."

"It is. That's the one acceptance. But here's the thing: when I e-mailed my submission, I forgot to include my bio. I was in a hurry to get it sent, and I only sent them the story. It's a miracle they even looked at it, because these places are usually pretty strict when it comes to following their submission guidelines."

"And?" she asked, unsure what he was getting at.

"And . . . that's the story that was accepted."

"I don't understand."

"They didn't know anything about me. They didn't know that I hadn't published anything before, or that I was just some dumb kid barely out of high school. They took my story seriously. They took *me* seriously."

"You're not saying that these places have been rejecting your work because of your age, are you?"

"It seemed awfully coincidental," he said. "But now . . ."

He held up the envelope. Sarah followed it with her eyes as he tossed it onto the bed.

"Now I don't know what to think," he finished.

"Is this something from a magazine?" she asked, picking it up. It was addressed to KEVIN REED, and when she turned it over she saw it wasn't opened.

"It's about my book," he said.

"Book?"

"A novel. I've been working on it for a couple of years."

"And this is someone writing you back about it?"

"I've been corresponding with a literary agent, who is someone who submits your book to publishing houses for you. A lot of publishers *only* work with agents, so it's often a necessity to have one. The problem is, it's really hard to get an agent and the process can take months, if not years." He pointed at the envelope. "Five months ago I tracked down an agent that represents books similar to mine, and I sent the first three chapters of my book to them. They wrote back saying they really liked the chapters, and they wanted me to send them the entire book. Which I did. Two months ago. I just figured they passed since I never heard anything back."

"When did you get this?" she asked.

"It came in the mail this morning. I shoved it into my pocket and promised myself I'd open it by the end of the day."

"I can't believe this," she said with a grin. "I get to be here when you get your big break. Here, open it."

She tried to hand it back to him, but he didn't take it. At first she thought he was messing with her, but all the color had gone out of his face, and he was wringing his hands together.

"Hey," she said, "no matter what this says, it doesn't change who you are. You wrote a freakin book. And you're going to write more books. If they don't want this one, they'll want the next one."

"But what if they hated it? What if they tell me I'm just a stupid kid who has no business writing anything? Who am I to have anything to say? Why should the world listen to me?"

"You've really been carrying this around all day?" she asked.

"Yeah. Will you open it for me?"

"Me?" She shook her head. "You don't mean that. This is yours. It's for you to open."

"Please?"

He was watching her with a wide-eyed, almost child-like stare. She nodded, waited another second to make sure he meant it, and slowly tore open the back flap. She slid out the letter. She read it twice carefully before committing to it verbally.

"Kevin . . ."

"Dammit," he said. "I knew—"

"They like it."

He looked up. "What?"

"Dear Mr. Reed," she read with a smile. "Please excuse this letter, but we have been unable to reach you by phone and our e-mails have gone unanswered. We're extremely excited about your project, *Errant Souls*, and we look forward to speaking with you at your earliest convenience." Her smile grew. "It's signed by Edgar Aust. There's a phone number to call."

Kevin took the letter and read for himself. Sarah felt her heart swell as a grin spread across his face.

"I can't believe it," he said. "I just . . . I can't believe it."

"*Believe* it. Even though I've never read anything you've written, I know you're a damn great writer. I get a signed copy after it's published, right?"

"Hold on a minute. This is just the first hurdle. The real trick is to see if they can actually get a publisher interested in it."

"They will," Sarah said with a smile. "No question."

Kevin let out his breath. "I had a teacher once tell me that if you have a little talent and want something badly enough, you can get it. I'm not naïve enough to think I'm on my way to fame and fortune . . . but to possibly get paid to do something I love? How incredible would that be?"

She bit her lip as a blush came over her face. A writer, a nice guy, good looking . . . it was all too good to be true.

"And now I have my reason," he said, his smile dimming. "My reason to leave."

"Leave?"

"I have a cousin who lives in Chicago. He's a few years older than me, but he's a good guy, and he knows what it's like to . . . have difficulty at home. We were close growing up, and every time I talk with him, he tells me I should come live with him once I've graduated."

"Oh," she said quietly.

"I can't stay in this town, Sarah. It would kill me to stay here. I don't want to be like my father. You get it, right? I'm not running away . . . I'm starting over. Starting my life."

"Sure," she said with a quick nod, feeling the sting of tears. "So that was the plan? Wake up some morning and drive away? Just like that?"

"Yeah," he said flatly, "pretty much. Outside of the clothes I carry with me, there's really nothing else to take. A few books. A laptop that's so old it barely works. My car has always felt more like home than my house. Chicago is no more than a day's drive. Once I cross the city limits, there's no looking back. My father probably won't even know I'm gone until the refrigerator runs out of food."

"That's great," she said. She swiped at her eyes with her palms. "I'm really happy for you. Excuse me."

She stood and went into the bathroom. Kevin rose from the chair as the door closed, and a moment later he could hear what sounded like crying from the other side. Crying for him. *Him.* A kid who had been called a "worthless piece of shit" by his father too many times to count. A kid with no money, no real friends, and a horrifying past. He could hardly believe it, but the proof was there, crying on the other side of the door.

He knocked softly. "Sarah?"

"Go if you're going," she said, her words thick with tears. "I'll be fine."

"Sarah, please come out and talk to me."

She didn't answer.

"I'm not leaving until you come out," he told her through the door. "I'll wait here until the morning if that's what it takes, because I need you to understand something. The things I've told you tonight . . . I've never told anyone that stuff. That's the sort of stuff a person keeps locked up inside, because once it's leaked from your mouth, you wonder how you survived at all. If you can keep it all hidden away, then you don't have to face it . . . and then you don't have to live with it. I have no business dumping my mess on you. No business at all. And I'm sorry for that. But I *wanted* to tell you, Sarah. A part of me needed to tell you."

He put his hand on the door.

"Earlier you said that sometimes bad things can just happen, and that's just the way it is. But you know what I also believe? I believe that sometimes *good* things can also happen. Like me finding you. That was a good thing. Do you believe that?"

He didn't expect her to answer, but he waited just the same.

"Yes," she replied. It was almost a whisper and he barely caught it.

"I like you, Sarah. Do you believe that?"

Pause. "Maybe."

He looked around the room and a small smile crossed his lips. "Is your purse in there with you?"

"Yes."

"Do you believe I got you a birthday present?"

Silence.

"Open your purse, Sarah. Look at the very bottom."

He wet his lips and waited. It felt like a long time before the door opened, and when it did, she was standing there with the silver chain and cross in her hand.

"How . . ."

"I knew you were special from the moment I saw you," he told her. "And I knew I would do anything to get to know you. Do you believe that?"

Tears began to shine her eyes. "Yes."

"I don't know what will happen tomorrow or the next day, and it doesn't matter, because you and I are here right now. Nothing can change that. No parents or boyfriends or letters . . . not *anything*."

For a moment she only stared, as if processing his words, and then she leaned forward and gently kissed him on the lips. His pulse quickened as she pulled away.

"Will you stay with me tonight?" she asked, her voice just above a whisper. "Just to sleep. That's all. Just . . . stay and hold me."

"Are you sure?"

"The only thing I've ever been sure of in my entire life," she replied carefully, "is this moment right now."

She went to the bed and slid under the sheets. Kevin removed his shoes and looked down at her with a smile. Her long hair was splayed across her pillow and her cheeks were glowing.

"Would it be corny to say you look like an angel?" he asked.

"Maybe," she said with a coy smile. "But I never believe compliments that come from writers. They get too much practice using words."

He said, "Only so they can use them at the right moment."

"Touché."

She snapped off the light as he climbed in beside her.

[32]

Scott stood trembling at the door with one eye glued to the peephole. Five minutes ago he had been on his way to get something to drink; five minutes ago he had peeked out through the drapes to make sure no one was around; five minutes ago he had seen someone moving inside the weight room across from the pool.

And now that someone was standing out in the open, staring back at him. Seeing him through the closed door.

"I don't know you," Scott whispered in a rickety voice.

The figure stood motionless, its head dipped forward and shadowed. Something long and twisted hung from its left hand. Scott tried to blink away the sweat from his eyes; tried to focus. Everything was a blur.

"Screw this," he said, breaking away from the door with a push. "Screw this and screw you."

He blindly grabbed for the phone, knocking it off the table and sending it to the floor. With a shaky hand he snatched it up and somehow managed to dial the lobby. It was probably just some drunken guy, trying to remember what room he belonged in. Mandy would take care of it.

"Come on," he hissed into the phone after the fourth ring.

Maybe she's dead, a voice whispered.

Scott felt his hand tighten around the receiver. The phone rang endlessly: five . . . six . . .

Maybe she's—

"She's not dead," Scott croaked.

But the thought stuck in his mind, scratching at the corners of his mind. Someone had been murdered on Chestnut Street, only two blocks away from the hotel. And Mandy worked the night shift alone, pissing off customers—

—like the man from the lobby.

The phone slipped from his fingers. He had forgotten about the man from earlier, the man who had threatened to cut Mandy's throat.

"It's not him," Scott whispered. "It could be anybody."

Anybody or anything . . .

An icy chill trickled down his spine. Scott felt his lips move; no words came through.

Your dad—

"—is dead," he finished.

A sound jerked his head and he let out a cry; the bathroom door was ajar and he could see a faint image of himself in the mirror. His other self stared back at him.

"My dad is dead," he said in a thin voice, "and it wasn't my fault."

His reflection made no movement as Scott spoke. He lifted his hand and his mirror image did not.

He bolted forward and slammed shut the bathroom door. It was the pills and his brain was on the verge of a shutdown from exhaustion; it was just more tricks of the mind.

It was the guilt that drove him to the brink of insanity, the voice whispered, *and he became so lost in his madness, he believed he was being haunted . . .*

"I'm not crazy," Scott rasped.

The goddamn man from the lobby and his bullshit stories—it wasn't real, none of it was real; it was all in his head and nothing was coming for him.

But something is out there—

"Nothing is out there!"

He raced back to the door and pushed his eye against the peephole. The figure was moving now, coming toward his room . . . coming for him . . .

Everything was on overload. His heart was thundering, trying to break out from his chest. A heart attack, he was going to have a heart attack, just like his dad—

—came back from the dead to take care of unfinished business—

"It wasn't my fault!" Scott screamed, spit flying from his mouth. "He's dead and it wasn't my fault!"

Returned the dead to punish him for his sin . . .

"Sarah," he whispered.

Sarah had been his last chance. His last chance to do something good in this world and redeem himself . . . and she had rejected him.

"Get Sarah!" Scott screeched. "Get her! It's her fault! Hers!"

He reached into his pocket and drew out the knife with a shuddering hand.

Maybe something inside you is broken, Mandy whispered.

Scott closed his eyes; everything went red.

• • •

Kevin bolted upright in the bed as their room window shattered in an eruption of glass. Before Sarah could shriek, Kevin was on his feet, wrestling his shirt back on.

"Stay down," he told her. Broken glass was everywhere, and in the middle of the floor he saw a rusty tire iron—the object that had broken the window.

"Get out here!" a voice boomed. "You get out here *right* now or I'm coming in!"

The drapes were still in place, blocking Kevin's line of vision, but he could hear someone moving outside, breathing in loud gasps of air. He grabbed the empty glass bottle of orange juice by its neck. It barely had any weight to it, but it was better than nothing. His heart accelerated as he unlocked the door and held the knob.

The person outside began to shout: "Three . . . two . . . one—"

Kevin whipped open the door and charged outside.

• • •

"Kevin!" Sarah screeched, throwing away the covers.

"I'll kill you!" a voice roared.

She clawed for the phone, knocking it from its stand. Outside the room there was thumping, shouting—a splintering crash.

"Don't!" someone cried.

Sarah fell to the floor, grabbed the phone, and punched out nine-one-one.

"Sarah!" another voice shouted.

Tears streamed down her cheeks as the phone beeped at her. She didn't dial a nine. The stupid nine . . .

The door flew open and Scotty was standing there with a glint of metal in his hand. It was covered in blood.

"Sarah?" he choked.

The phone slipped from her fingers.

"I didn't mean it," Scotty said, his words dissolving into a string of sobs. "I thought . . . I didn't . . . I did it for you . . ."

Sarah began to scream.

AFTER

"Just start at the beginning," the officer told her. "All we want to do is figure out exactly what happened."

Sarah nodded and held the tissue against her mouth. "He was trying to protect me. I just want to make sure that's clear."

"I'll take it all down," the officer assured her.

Her eyes drifted to Scotty, who was standing hunched over, his hair hanging down and covering his face. His hands were bound behind him with handcuffs.

"Sarah?" the officer prodded.

She told him how she and Matt were stranded, how she and Kevin had met, and everything that happened while they were looking for Scotty. When she reached the part about checking into the hotel, the officer stopped her.

"Your mother filled in some information here . . ." He flipped back a few pages and read from the pad: "Your mother was out looking for you when you called home. When she returned, she got your message and was relieved that you were okay. She knew who Scotty was."

"Scotty's an old friend of the family," Sarah said.

"Shortly after that, Matt showed up at your house looking for you. Your mother played the message for him, and he said he was happy you were safe and said he was going home. Matt admitted to your mother the two of you had had a small argument, but he promised your mother everything would be okay in the morning. But now we know that Matt didn't go back home. At this point Matt proceeded here to the hotel, only knowing that you were in some room with some other guy."

The officer flipped forward again in his pad.

"What happened next is still unclear," he went on. "More than an hour passed between the time Matt left your house and showed up here at the hotel. What do you think happened in that time?"

"I have no idea."

"Earlier you stated that Matt was intoxicated. Is it possible that he stopped off somewhere to drink some more? A bar, maybe? Is it possible that he slowly worked himself into a frenzy, thinking of his girlfriend at some hotel with a guy he didn't know?"

"I don't know," Sarah replied, slightly confused. "Is that important?"

"Look, I have a boy in handcuffs and a boy in the hospital. We can piece together how it happened, but that doesn't explain why it happened. If I can place him—Matt—at a bar, I can accept that he was drunk and didn't know what he was doing. I can work with that."

She was startled by the frankness of his voice—for the first time he actually sounded like a person instead of a dictating machine—but she still had no answers to give.

"I'm sorry," she said. "I don't know."

He sighed. "Another theory is that Matt *did* come straight to the hotel but wasn't sure what room you were in. The female desk clerk never saw him, but she did receive a call that someone suspicious was wandering around the hotel. That was probably Matt looking for you. Did you leave your room after checking in?"

Sarah thought carefully before answering. "Yes. A couple times. Mostly to use the vending machines."

"And again, time passed before Matt made contact and broke the window with the tire iron. We have to assume he spotted you when you left the room, so what reason would he have to wait?"

She paused again, trying to make an answer for him that he would understand. "It had to be on his terms," was all she could say. She dumped her eyes to the floor and shivered.

The officer waited a moment, and when it became apparent she had no more to offer, he scribbled in his pad and turned his head. "Why don't *you* tell me what happened after the window broke."

Kevin said, "We were inside the room when something crashed through the window and shattered the glass. I immediately assumed it was Scott and that he had thrown something."

"But it was Matt," the officer said.

"Yes," Kevin agreed. "And when I went out the door—"

"And why exactly did you think it was a good idea to confront whoever was out there? What did you think you were going to do?"

"Make sure that no one hurt Sarah," Kevin answered without pause. The officer jotted in his pad and motioned for Kevin to continue.

"I went out the door and saw some guy—Matt—getting ready to come at me with raised fists. That was when Scott burst out of the room next to ours and charged straight for Matt. At first I thought Scott was punching him . . ."

Kevin wiped a shaky hand across his mouth. Sarah wrapped her arm around his waist.

"I thought that Scott was punching him, but then I realized . . . I saw the knife come up, and I realized Scott was *stabbing* him."

"Seven times," the officer said, and cleared his throat. "Scott says he thought it was something else. Not someone, but *something*. What do you think he means by that?"

"All I know," Sarah said, "is that I believe Scotty thought he was saving me."

The officer shot a glance over to Scott. "Seven times is a lot of saving. It doesn't look good for him, whatever his reasoning. He's going to jail for assault and possession of illegal drugs. As far as I'm concerned, he was high and didn't know what he was doing. That seems like the only clear cut thing in this whole ordeal."

"What about Matt?" Sarah asked.

"He'll be brought up on destruction of property—"

"I mean . . . will he be okay?"

"You can check on him at the hospital. I don't have any information." He shut the notebook with a snap. "I think I have everything I need for the moment. Excuse me."

"Wait," Sarah said as the officer turned to leave. "Can I have a minute with Scotty?"

The officer frowned but nodded. "*One* minute."

Scott was still staring into the ground, and when she touched him on the shoulder his head turned up.

"Scott?"

"I messed up again," he said under his breath. He looked in her direction, and tears began to water his eyes. "I didn't mean to mess up."

"I know," she said gently.

"Do you hate me, Sarah?"

"No," she whispered. "No, Scott, I don't hate you at all."

A long sob escaped his mouth. She reached out and brushed the hair from his eyes.

"I heard you talking," Scott whispered. "Do you think Matt was going to hurt you?"

"I don't know," she said softly.

He stared at her, blinking heavily against the flow of tears. "But he could have, right? He could have hurt you."

She thought back to Matt standing on the road with her at the beginning of the night: *If you leave me, I'll make you very sorry.*

Scott said, "So doesn't that mean this all could be a *good* thing?"

"Let's go," the officer said, grabbing Scott by the arm.

"Doesn't that count for something?" Scott cried, almost pleading. "Doesn't that *mean* something?"

He began to struggle, and Sarah cupped her hands over her mouth. The officer jerked up on the handcuffs and Scott gave a strangled cry as he was dragged around the corner. Kevin touched her shoulder and she jumped, startled by the touch.

"You okay?" he asked.

She didn't answer. She began to walk after Scott, slowly at first, then with more speed. A police cruiser was parked outside the lobby doors, and through the window she saw Scott slouched forward in the back seat. She went to the cruiser and placed her hand on the glass.

"Scott."

He was crying now, his head bobbing up and down.

"Scotty!" she said, tapping on the glass. The engine roared to life and she shouted his name again. The cruiser clunked into gear and Scott rolled his head toward her, his eyes wide and unsettled.

"Yes, Scotty," she said, nodding. "Yes. It means something."

A smile broke apart his face as tears flooded his cheeks. Somehow she found a smile of her own and gave it to him. The cruiser pulled out of the parking lot and onto the street.

He was gone.

She turned and Kevin was there. "They'd like us to go down to the station," he said.

"What time is it? I'm afraid to know." She held out her arm so he could see her watch. "Just tell me if it's early or late."

"It's early."

She slid into his arms and he began to stroke her hair.

"The night's almost gone then," she whispered. "What happens in the morning?"

"I don't know," he answered quietly.

She drew back and looked into his eyes. "How does the story end, the one with the two people?"

It seemed like an eternity before he spoke, and when he did, it was barely a whisper. "I don't know that either."

"Does he leave?"

"Sarah . . ."

She pulled into him tightly, afraid to ask any other questions.

"Let's go back inside and wait," he said.

They went through the doors together, and she told herself she wasn't going to cry anymore.

All the tears inside her were gone.

• • •

Kody turned over the last page and set the manuscript on the grass beside him. The color in the sky felt wrong, and a glance at his watch told him he had been reading for the better part of four hours.

"Lost time," he muttered as he stood.

Sabrina was propped against a neighboring tree with her fingers curled around a paperback. When she saw him coming, she lowered the book into her lap and immediately began to tug at a strand of loose hair.

"Don't forget to bite your lip," he said.

"Funny. *Well?*"

"Patience," he said, sitting beside her. "You wouldn't let me peek at it once while you were writing it."

"That's my style. Now tell me what you think."

He randomly began flipping pages. "You didn't make me very dashing. And where did you come up with the name Kevin?"

She tittered. "He was a boy in grade school that would wipe boogers on my shirt when I wasn't looking. The names have to be changed to protect the innocent, you know."

"Yeah, but *Kevin*? That's like a wussy name."

She gave him a peck on the cheek. "No one is more wussy than you, babe. Sorry."

"I love it," he said, squeezing her leg. "Who knew you had the makings of a great writer inside you?"

"You did. Besides, I had some pretty heavy inspiration for the story. What time are you talking with your agent again tomorrow?"

"Nine. He thinks Mullikin Books may be ready to make a firm offer. The advance probably won't be much, but it's something."

She batted her eyes. "And you'll mention your lovely girlfriend and her first novel?"

"Find your own damn publisher," he said with a grin. "I'm not peddling the competition."

"Says you!" she laughed, poking him repeatedly in the stomach. "You like that, punk? Do ya?"

He caught her hands. "Your kung fu fingers are no match for the titty-twister—"

"We're in public!" she cried, pulling away. "And I made that part up!"

"Yeah," he said with a sigh, "all the juicy stuff is never true. But you could have at least given me rippling muscles."

"Uh, not even fiction can lie about everything."

He smiled at her. "Do you really expect everyone to believe it all happened that way?"

She fingered the silver cross that lay across her neck. "They may *believe* what they like . . ."

He began to tickle her then, and they giggled in the fading light of Millennium Park.

AUTHOR'S NOTE

Thanks so much for reading ROAM. It's an odd little book that I wrote in my twenties, and even after all these years, I still have a soft spot in my heart for Kevin, Sarah, and yes—even Scotty, who was based on a childhood friend. I miss you, Kirby.

If you enjoyed ROAM, please take a moment to leave a **review** at Amazon or Goodreads. It doesn't have to be long or fancy; anything is good. Thanks again for reading and stay safe!

Read an excerpt from Erik Therme's

IF SHE DIES

I slouch further into the driver's seat as Eve exits her apartment complex across the street. Today, she's wearing jean shorts, sandals, and a blue tank top; blonde hair pulled into a crooked ponytail, her electric-pink backpack secured firmly over both shoulders. Eve turned twelve a few weeks ago, and since that day, she walks the six blocks to and from Chandler Middle School alone. Today, she's a few minutes later than yesterday, but last Friday she was so early I almost missed her leaving. That won't happen again.

Eve stops just outside the complex doors and tilts her head upward. Her mother, Meg, is raining down an angry stream of words from the screen-less window one story above. I can't make out what's being said, but I do manage to catch a single word riding the mild May breeze: *ungrateful.* There was clearly an argument this morning, maybe about laundry that wasn't folded, or unfinished homework, or a dishwasher that wasn't unloaded, or one of a thousand other things a mother raising a twelve-year-old daughter alone can stress over.

But Eve is a trooper.

She patiently listens to every word with her head raised, not talking back, not crossing her arms, not reflecting her mother's anger. I think to myself: what if today's the day? What if something unthinkable happens to Eve this very morning and she's never seen again? What would Meg do with that guilt? How would she live with herself, knowing her final words to her daughter were angry and bitter over something trivial and inconsequential?

As if reading my thoughts, Meg abruptly stops and brushes her long, knotty hair from her face as she straightens. A woman has exited the complex; fifty, maybe sixty years old, and I lean sideways in my seat, trying to see past the motorcycle that has pulled into the space directly in front of my car, partially blocking my view. The driver is a pudgy, fifty-something man on a Harley Davidson that's undoubtedly feeding his mid-life crisis. I debate getting out so I can see across the street, but I can't risk drawing attention to myself. As long as I stay inside my car, people will remember nothing more than an aging Chevy Malibu in the parking lot of JoKat Coffee, killing time before driving to work, or maybe waiting for someone who's still inside. Fortunately, the motorcycle man is quick to dismount, stowing his helmet on the seat and sauntering toward the coffee shop entrance without so much as a glance in my direction.

The older woman is now talking with Eve and invading her personal space by several inches. She's a friend . . . no—a neighbor, stopping to make sure everything's okay. She lives on the same floor, maybe even in the apartment across from them, and doesn't like when Eve and her mother argue. Maybe she's a lonely widow who lingers just inside her door, listening for Eve and Meg as they come and go so she can "coincidentally" bump into them for a moment of human contact. Once a month, she makes cookies—horrible raisin or bran cookies that have been baked from recipes in her family for generations—and dutifully marches them across the hallway to Eve and Meg, hoping to be invited in for a few moments, maybe even invited to stay for dinner.

Eve is respectful and quiet as the woman says what she has to say, and when I shift my gaze to the upstairs window, Meg is gone. The woman smiles, pats Eve on the shoulder, and goes on her way in the opposite direction.

I start my car's engine.

Eve ambles down the sidewalk with her hands locked around the straps of her backpack and her golden ponytail swaying with each step. Traffic is in full swing this time of morning, and by the time I'm able to maneuver a left turn out of the parking lot, Eve has disappeared around the corner onto Bickerstaff. It doesn't worry me. I know where she's going.

I drive west on Merritt, passing Enmon's Bakery, until I turn north onto Davis, less than two miles from where Lily Jean bled out in my arms. I still see her pale face every single day, staring up at me, begging—pleading for help—as I watch her die.

Grady Park is just ahead.

The playground is fairly quiet with only a few toddlers and a handful of joggers refilling water bottles from the drinking fountain. The park is adjacent to Chandler Middle School, connected by a green space half the size of a football field. There's a few empty spots in the lot, but I park on the street facing away from the school, pointed in the opposite direction.

I keep my head down as I trek the short distance to the park. There's two covered shelters—one on each side of the play equipment—along with a smattering of individual picnic tables. I choose one nearest the school and away from the chaos of feral children, which gives me a clear shot of the front entrance to Chandler. The beginning of the school day is in motion, and I watch parents shoo children from cars; students playfully grab things from each other's hands, and teachers drag themselves into the building, dreading the school day ahead.

And then: Eve.

I'm too far away to see the exact features of her face, but she's laughing with her friends and making exaggerated gestures, as if acting out something for a laugh. She looks happy, but it's only an illusion. On the inside, she's not okay. We're the same in that way. And because of that, our paths are unavoidable.

My cell phone vibrates on the table like a convulsing insect. The screen says JOSH—I've been expecting his call—and I mechanically put the phone to my ear without taking my eyes from Eve.

"It's me," Josh says. "Are you in Newton?"

"Yes," I reply. The word barely leaves my lips.

There's a pause, and then: "Did she see you?"

Eve is chatting with classmates—a boy and two girls—and I catch a glimpse of her face as she turns toward the park, as if knowing something isn't right but unsure what it might be. The girl beside her, tall with braces, tugs on Eve's backpack to get her to move. Eve follows her into the school and disappears.

"Yes," I lie.

There's another pause, longer this time, and I can visualize Josh inside his office in Delmar, leaning forward in his plush leather chair, fidgeting with a pen. His desk is tidy with every paperclip and Post-It Note in its place, and the stapler is perfectly aligned with the tape dispenser.

"Good," he says. I hear the creak of his chair as he leans back, settling in to the conversation neither of us wants to have. We haven't spoken since our argument last night after dinner, which wasn't as much an argument as it was a scolding. Josh rarely raises his voice at me, and his words still ring in my ears like tinnitus. He's frustrated with me, and I understand. I would be too. That's why I promised him I would drive into Newton today and try to make an appointment with the therapist my physician recommended. I want to be a good wife. I do. But I also know that seeing a therapist isn't the answer. There's no fix for my problem.

"Today was only a preliminary meeting," I tell him. Lying comes easily to me now. "We only met for a few minutes, and I filled out a questionnaire and submitted our insurance information. She said she should be able to fit me into her schedule soon and would give me a call."

"That's great," Josh says almost sheepishly. He clears his throat, and I can hear him shift in his chair. "I'm . . . sorry about last night, Tess."

The apology hangs in the air. I want to believe he means it, that he's not just saying it because he got his way or because he knows he should say it, but I don't know anymore.

"I'm sorry too," I echo. I don't exactly know what I'm apologizing for, but I know it's the fastest way to get through the moment. He'll fill in the blanks, whether he believes it's me apologizing for not seeing things his way, or maybe me apologizing for being depressed, as if that's something I can simply turn off and on like a switch.

But I get it. It's been almost nine months. He's moved on. I haven't. In his mind, a therapist can magically fix me, and things can go back to the way they were before. He truly believes this.

"I thought I'd leave early tonight," he says. "Grab a pizza for dinner."

Josh never, *ever* leaves early from work. He always arrives home promptly at six thirty; never goes into the office late; never takes sick days. Something is definitely up—more than just trying to make amends for an argument.

I realize I haven't answered him, and I force a smile. It's a trick I learned long ago; forcing yourself to smile changes the tone of your words, if not your mind-set.

"Pizza sounds great," I tell him.

"Good. And good luck job hunting today," he adds. "Hopefully, something looks interesting."

I smile again, but this time without comment. Last week, Josh scoured the local online want-ads and e-mailed me a handful of places currently hiring in Newton; entry level jobs such as a copy technician at a printing house, and cashier at an organic food market. I haven't worked in over six years, and my BA in Communications didn't exactly open a ton of doors for me back then.

Therapy + Job = Old Tess Parker.

My husband is an optimist.

Josh is speaking again, but it's not to me; someone has entered his office. I wait patiently as he exchanges a few muffled words, followed by *Be right there*.

"I have to go, Tess. Can't wait to hear how the job search goes. See you tonight."

And then he's gone. No goodbye, no I love you; only a dead line. There was a time when my husband said those three words to me every day, but I can't remember the last time I heard them.

They're only words, I tell myself.

The schoolyard is quiet, the students safe within the

walls. It's a few minutes after eight, which means Eve will reappear at twelve fifteen after finishing lunch, then again at three when school is dismissed. Her return walk home is always leisurely, unhurried, and always alone—Russell to Brighton, then Allen, then Dickerson. Eve's apartment complex has a small courtyard with plastic lounge chairs, and once Eve has deposited her backpack upstairs, she always returns outside with a book and a snack and settles herself into a lounger, sometimes for hours on end.

I know this, because Eve has followed this routine every day now for the last three weeks. I also know that Eve's mother, Meg, has been working second shift at the movie theater for the last two weeks, leaving Eve home alone in the evenings, sometimes as late as eleven or midnight.

It's not right that Meg gets to keep her daughter while mine was taken away from me. It's not right that Eve gets to live while my Lily does not.

Someone has to right this wrong.

Made in the USA
Monee, IL
08 July 2026

56679417R00142